I0597262

THE PSYCHIC

A SORCERER'S AWAKENING

JOHN IOVINE

ISBN 978-1-62385-026–5 E-Book
ISBN 978-1-62385-032-6 Print

Table of Contents

Chapter 1 - Revelation

I sank into my leather recliner, its frame solid, the stitching fine, the cushions molding to me, like they'd known my shape for years. The hide was warm under my palms, the intoxicating scent of expensive leather mixed faintly with the sharp, woody smell of oak. I slipped off my loafers, swirled Glenfiddich in a snifter, and took a slow sip. The only sound was the measured tick of the grandfather clock.

BANG! BANG! BANG!

The glass jerked in my hand. Scotch splashed down my silk shirt, stinging where it hit skin. "Son of a bitch!" I grabbed a tissue from the desk, blotting at the damage…pointless. The pounding didn't stop; it continued to rattle down the hallway.

"I'm coming!" My socks slid on polished wood as I tore toward the front door. I yanked it open. "What?"

A thirty-something man pulled back; his face was pale and gaunt, eyes red and swollen. His cheap, ill-fitting suit was rumpled, and the tails of his shirt were pulled out of his trousers. He cleared his throat.

"I need your help! Someone kidnapped my son." His voice cracked; he took a breath. "Please," he said, pushing a child's blue sports jersey to me. "Can you see where he is and if he's okay?"

Now, this is what we in the business call a problem. I placed my hand over his as he clutched the jersey. His skin was clammy and damp from perspiration. "I'm sorry about your son; I can't get involved without being brought in by the police -- legalities, like impeding an investigation."

He smelled of sweat and nerves – his face held a combination of anxiety, fear, and frustration.

"Legalities?" He repeated. His voice tightened. "I'll take full responsibility. This is my son's life."

I couldn't afford to take part of a police investigation - that could confirm I was a fake. I backpedaled. "Psychic phenomena are not like a light you can turn on and off with a switch. You have the best chance of finding your son by working with the police."

He grimaced and wiped his eyes. I felt for him, but what option did I have? I couldn't confess I wasn't a real psychic. If that got out, I'd be ruined.

"Please," he said. "You have to try. My wife's been with the police all afternoon. Any chance with you is better than no chance at all." He shook the vibrant blue jersey in his clenched fist.

I sensed he was moments away from a meltdown, so I nodded. "Please, come in. I'll give it a try."

He said his name was James Carter. James handed me the jersey with the number five printed in bold white letters on the front. "Johnny wore it yesterday."

He followed me into my den. I sat in my recliner, closed my eyes, and breathed deeply, imitating a trance mode. This wasn't a lost cat or cheating spouse. So, I did my best double-mumbo-jumbo act for two minutes before deeply exhaling and standing.

"I'm sorry, I'm not getting anything," I said solemnly, handing back the boy's jersey. I brightened my voice and said, "Check with your wife; maybe there's good news."

He frowned. "Are you for real?" he asked.

I was surprised James asked me this question, considering the circumstances. I may be a fake, but I'm an expert fake, thank you very much. I repeated my canned response reserved for such questions of authenticity. "Yes, I've been tested by reputable university scientists in double-blind tests."

"So, you're psychic and not just a magic act?" he asked, his voice hardening.

"Psychic, yes," I confirmed with a nod, feeling a knot tightening in my stomach.

He glanced around the room, his eyes cold and calculating. "You live alone?"

"What?" I stammered, caught off guard by the abrupt change in tone.

"Do you live alone?" he repeated, more insistent this time, his gaze locking onto mine.

A chill raced down my spine. "Yeah, why?" I managed, my throat tightening.

He reached into his suit pocket and pulled out a gun. He leveled the gun at me. I froze, my world narrowing to that single point of black-metal barrel two inches from the tip of my nose. "Help me find my son," he growled, his voice low and deadly, "or I'll blow your fucking brains out."

I held my hands up instinctively. "You're upset. Let me explain."

"Shut the fuck up!" James pushed the gun barrel hard against my forehead. "I don't care what you have to do. Contact your spirit guide, pray to God, or summon your demon lover. Help me or die!"

"I'll help." I spat the words out.

"Good choice!" His lips twisted into a grim smile. "Put your hands down, and let's go. My car is parked across the street."

"Can I put my shoes on?" I asked.

"Do it."

I grabbed my Italian loafers, my hand quivering as I lifted my scotch and downed what was left in the glass.

■■

Outside, the night air was a slap of reality. James beeped his car alarm, the sound echoed in the quiet street. When he opened the door, the nauseating stench of McDonald's fast-food wafted out. The car's dome light revealed crumpled wrappers, empty cups, and a few desiccated French fries leaning out of a cup holder. The backseat held a pile of children's sports equipment.

I hesitated.

"Get in!" he barked, jamming his gun into my ribs. "You drive."

Reluctantly, I slid into the driver's seat. My trousers were sticking to some unknown residue. James got in on the passenger side and jammed his key into the ignition.

"Okay, how do we start?" he asked, clicking his seat belt.

I turned away from him, trying to separate myself from whatever was glued to my pants. "Do you ever clean this car?"

I caught a glimpse of the gun arcing towards me before smashing into my skull. The expression "I saw stars" is not far from the truth.

"Don't worry about the fucking car." He roared. "Worry about finding my son."

I winced, rubbing my forehead. A bump was already swelling. *Not now,* I told myself *stay alive first, but soon, you bastard, I'll be testifying against you in court.* "Give me his clothes," I grunted.

The first rule of faking psychic abilities is reducing client expectations. So, I began my usual script, "I can't guarantee anything. I can only provide whatever psychic impressions I receive. This is the process. Do you understand?" I said, trying to establish some rapport.

James shook his head, eyes ice-cold. "No, you understand. If my son winds up dead in a ditch somewhere, I'm putting you in beside him."

I nodded. *That didn't go as well as I'd hoped.* Glancing toward my neighbor's house, I caught the flicker of a TV through the window. *Was there any way to contact them?* "I need a few minutes," I said, stalling for time, my mind searching for an opportunity.

"I swear to God if you're jerking me around." He pressed the gun against my temple, the cold metal punctuating his threat.

Sweat trickled down my forehead. "Threats are making it harder for me to focus; I need to concentrate if I am to help you find your son." Closing my eyes, I buried my face in the boy's jersey, inhaling the odors of sweat and grass with a hint of the detergent used to wash it. I hoped that this looked like I was making a psychic connection. I couldn't think of anything to say, and I didn't want to get anything wrong.

I emptied my mind of thoughts and breathed deeply. A blue Chevy Malibu flashed in my mind's eye, like the car I'd owned in college.

"Is a blue car involved?" I asked, drawing out the words slowly.

James's eyes widened. "Yes, a blue car!" James cried out. "A witness told the cops they saw my son Johnny leaving with a man in one."

I leaned in with the jersey still covering my face, shifting it just enough to peek at James. "I'm seeing planes... taking off and landing," I spoke as if describing a scene from some psychic imagery. I stole another peek; James was jumping in his seat.

"The airport," James said.

I lowered the jersey from my face and nodded.

James pointed the gun toward the ignition. "Let's go. Newark Airport is the closest."

"I can't maintain a psychic connection and drive at the same time," I said.

His eyes narrowed as he squinted at me. He took a few moments, but he finally nodded. "All right," he grunted, and we swapped places. James took the wheel, and I slid into the passenger side.

Good, I thought, *much harder to shoot me while driving.*

As if reading my mind, he said, "I can shoot you just as easily from here. I don't even have to aim. So don't get any ideas."

"How will shooting me help you find your son?"

He cursed me under his breath.

Undeterred, I said, "Focus on driving, not me."

James veered onto the Staten Island Expressway, heading to New Jersey. I shut my eyes, feeling the baseball jersey in my lap, and contemplated my next move.

After a few miles, my stomach knotted; I felt we were traveling in the wrong direction. This made no sense. My ruse was to get us to an airport, distract him, tip off airport security, and escape. The air grew heavier; sweat rolled from my brow, and the sharp pain in my stomach twisted deeper with each passing second.

"We're going the wrong way," I spat out, shocked at the sound of my own voice. Outside, the green and white highway sign leading to the Goethals Bridge loomed overhead.

"What? You said the airport. Newark's the closest airport," James snapped.

"Turn around." The cramps spread into my lower bowels. I doubled over in my seat, struggling to hold everything in.

James drove off the next exit, then merged back onto the expressway in the opposite direction.

"Now what?" James growled.

"Just drive, God damn it." I snapped.

"Fucking great." James slammed his hand against the steering wheel.

My lips drew tight across my teeth -- "Listen, drop me off anywhere if you don't want my help."

James raised the gun in his right hand and pointed the barrel at me while his eyes remained fixed on the expressway. "Help? You're only helping me because of this." He poked the barrel into my side. I stayed silent, then he poked me harder. "I had to pull a gun on you for you to help me, right?" he yelled.

"Right," I admitted. "But I'm helping you now. I'm giving you everything I got. I can't do anything more."

James nodded, lowering the gun into his lap but keeping his fingers wrapped tightly around the grip. "Just don't bullshit me," James said, steering with one hand, his knuckles white on the wheel.

After a few minutes, the knot in my stomach slowly unraveled. I released my death grip on the jersey and placed it on the console between us, my fingers aching from the strain. Grateful for the relief, I exhaled and relaxed. We sped eastbound, heading toward Brooklyn.

As we passed the Victory Boulevard exit, James spoke. "We're five minutes from the Verrazano Bridge. Where are we going?"

I grabbed Johnny's baseball jersey. The moment my hand touched the fabric, my heart skipped a beat, then pounded. "Okay, something's up with this," I said.

James's head pivoted to me. I ignored him squeezing the material; it felt slick beneath my fingers. I focused on clearing my mind of thoughts.

But I couldn't empty my mind. I took a couple of deep breaths and concentrated on breathing. The shirt's fabric shifted from silky smooth to oily then slipped back to nothing. *What is happening here?* Frustrated, I scratched my head hard. I re-focused on my breath, and the oily sensation returned.

"Do you smell gasoline?" I asked.

James kept his eyes forward. "No."

A wave of dizziness hit, and the world tilted. Suddenly I was lying on my side, jolted with each bounce, ribs aching, head cracking against something hard. I couldn't see anything. I couldn't move; my wrists and ankles were tied. Then, some 1950s music faded in. "And now for all you cool cats in radio land, here's Fats Domino, 'Ain't That a Shame.'""

Panic surged. "I'm tied up in the trunk of a car; the car is moving," I shouted to James from within my vision. "It's hard to breathe."

I sensed the boy's heart pumping hard, my heart racing to catch up. When our hearts synchronized, I began to tremble as the boy did, trapped inside the trunk. My eyes burned with tears that weren't my own.

I tried to open my eyes, but everything remained black, and I couldn't move. I strained against the ropes binding my wrists and ankles together. Again and again, I bucked against the rope. The coarse fibers cut into my wrists, but I didn't stop struggling. Then, the resistance disappeared; my arms sprung up, slamming into the car's roof. Without thinking, I threw the jersey to the side.

The car swerved wildly -- first left, then right, tires squealing against the asphalt. Horns blared around us. My sight returned in time to see James rip the jersey from his face, cursing and throwing it aside.

"What the hell just happened!" James shouted, regaining control of the car.

I blinked, my breath short. "I'm not sure," I answered honestly.

"You stupid bastard," he spat. "Some psychic you are."

I thought back to when I was a kid; I could always find things - lost keys, rings, papers, jewelry, you name it. The lost thing tugged at me, drawing me toward it. The grown-ups were amazed at my ability, calling it a gift. But my father said the adults were only playing a joke on me. He said it wasn't real.

Even so, psychic phenomena continued to draw me to it. My father mocked me whenever he caught me reading a book or watching a TV show on the subject. And when I enrolled in a psychic school, he tore into me. But this time, his criticism happened to be correct. They offered little information on real psi phenomena. Instead, the school taught me how to do cold readings, size up a client by their appearance, and look for clues in their responses to my comments. It felt cheap and hollow. But what is happening now? I wasn't so sure.

        "Where are we going?" James asked, snapping me out of my thoughts.

        I glanced up; we were halfway across the Verrazano-Narrows Bridge. Instinctively, I reached for the jersey, clutching it in one hand, I swept my free hand slowly in front of me, probing for a direction. There -- a subtle pull to the right.

        "Go that way," I said, pointing to the Belt Parkway exit.

        "To Kennedy Airport? You're sure?"

        "No," I admitted, "but that's the impression I'm getting."

        I placed the jersey between us as James merged onto the bridge's exit and continued onto the Belt Parkway toward Kennedy Airport.

        Twenty minutes crawled by in silence, broken only by the thrum of the tires and hum of the engine. Then James spoke. "We're a quarter mile from the airport."

        I eyed the jersey resting on the car seat between us. My hand trembled as I reached for it, every nerve tight with hesitation. I rubbed my fingers on the satin material and meditated.

The impressions hit me hard - no slow fade in—no sensation of movement. Instead, I found myself lying in dirt, tall wet grass brushing against my skin. The scent of the wet earth mixed with burning wood filled the air. A small campfire crackled a few feet away from me, its yellow flames flickering upward, throwing glowing embers into the night sky. I couldn't move. My hands and feet were tied, and a gag stuffed into my mouth.

Across the fire, a man stood with his back to me. Denim overalls, heavy black boots, and a grease-stained tee shirt. He was pissing into the tall grass.

"Be with you in a second, boy. You're my bitch tonight." The man spoke in a thick, Southern drawl, and his voice was as rough as gravel.

My stomach clenched, cold fear shot up my spine and I trembled.

"Oh no," I snapped back into the car. "This is not good." I looked at James.

James shot me a glance. "Tell me."

"They're in a grass field."

"Look around for a landmark." James ordered, his eyes focused on the road.

I grabbed the jersey and submerged. I saw landing lights on the horizon and heard the drone of a propeller aircraft, its engine growing louder as it neared.

"They're by the airport," I said, my pulse quickening.

"Which way?" James pressed.

I closed my eyes, scanning my arm back and forth in an arc until I sensed a subtle tug.

"That way," I said, pointing toward Kennedy Airport.

James sped onto Rockland Boulevard. I glanced at my wristwatch: 8:30 p.m. Johnny had been kidnapped five and a half hours ago. The minutes felt heavier, time was slipping away. James skidded to a stop at an intersection.

"Which way?" he asked, his voice tense.

I did my scanning thing and felt a tug. "Turn right," I directed.

The road narrowed as we drove, running parallel to the airport. The desolate street was littered with unadorned metal buildings, cold and lifeless. As we drove, the buildings were replaced with For Sale signs on vacant lots. To our right, the lights from Kennedy airport shimmered through the tall grass.

"Grass fields -- we're close. Grab the jersey," James commanded.

I touched the jersey, the world around me shifted and I found myself pulled back into the nightmare. The man's knee dug painfully into my left shoulder as my arm was stretched upwards. The kidnapper locked my wrist in one hand while holding a cigarette in the other. He lowered the glowing cigarette toward my arm. I jerked away. He yelled, "Don't... fight... me...," his breath stank of rotten teeth and cheap alcohol. He brought the lit end of the cigarette down on my forearm. I screamed.

I tried to wrestle my arm away. He dug his knee deeper into my shoulder and pulled my arm out further. I could feel the joint straining on the verge of bursting out of its socket. I gave up and stopped struggling. He brought the cigarette down again. The stench of my burning skin made me gag, but I kept my arm limp, it was the only way to survive.

"That's right, you're my bitch. You want this, don't you?" He puffed the cigarette, bringing the smoldering tip back to life and brought it down on my arm.

My mind raced as I lay on the ground naked and vulnerable. This isn't real, I told myself. I am not here. I am in a car by Kennedy Airport. I must get back to the car.

But the pain was real. He leaned over me, his face twisted into a cruel smile, "You're prettier than a ten-year-old girl with your britches down," he taunted.

When I thought things couldn't get any worse, he spoke again. "When I'm done putting my mark on you, we'll have some real fun. You ain't never gonna forget tonight."

My heart raced at the threat and thought of what was to come. With great effort, I tossed the jersey to the side and returned to the car.

"I'm back."

"What happened?"

"He's marking your son with a cigarette; when he's finished, he's going to rape him."

"What! We have to find him -- we have to!" He spoke rapidly, his head jerked toward me, then back to the road.

I winced as my forearm throbbed. "I can feel that bastard's cigarette burns on my arm!" I pulled up my sleeve and found half of a pentagram burned into my forearm. "Fuck! Look." I turned my blistered arm toward James.

James's face paled at the sight of my injuries. "Did that just happen?" The car swerved wildly.

"Yes! God damn it," I yelled, "in the field with your son."

James struggled to keep his eyes on the road, turning his head to look at the blisters on my arm.

Am I going mad? The visions felt so real, and the burns, they're undeniable. James could see them too. As we approached a fork in the road, James turned to me for direction.

"Should I turn here?" James asked, gesturing toward a less traveled road to the right.

"I don't know." I shook my head.

James grabbed the jersey and held it out to me urgently. "Look."

I pushed the jersey back. I had enough. "No, I almost didn't make it back."

James dropped the jersey and raised his gun, pointing the barrel at my face.

"Pick up the fucking shirt and look," James commanded.

"Listen," I begged, "I think I'm hallucinating."

"Look at your arm – that's not a hallucination?"

"Maybe it's psychosomatic," I reasoned.

"Pick up the goddamn shirt," James ordered.

"I'm a fake," I confessed, voice cracking. "I'm sorry, I led you on."

James's eyes darkened. "No. You're lying. This is real. We're here."

"I can't go again," I said, my heart pounding. "I'm afraid I'll lose my mind completely. If you want to shoot me, go ahead, but I'm not going back."

James glanced at my forearm and pivoted the gun. BOOM! The muzzle flash lit the car's interior, and the window behind me shattered. I jumped. My ears rang, drowning out everything but the pounding in my chest. James aimed the gun back toward my head.

"Last chance," he said, voice barely audible through the ringing.

"You crazy fucking bastard." I spat, hands trembling as I grabbed the jersey. As soon as I closed my eyes, the darkness swallowed me, I fell back, descending in slow motion until I hit bottom. "I'm in the trunk again, but we're not moving," I reported.

James asked, "Which way?"

I swept my hand. I felt a tug in front of me. "Straight," I muttered.

We drove on, the gravel crunching beneath us until the road bent sharply left. As we rounded the corner, our headlights illuminated another car, parked in the tall grass, a few hundred feet ahead. Before I could speak, the car's headlights flared to life, and the vehicle jerked onto the road.

"Is that them?" James asked, his voice tense.

"Maybe. Wait, is that a blue car?"

James floored the accelerator. The back tires spun as our car fishtailed to the left. The engine screamed in protest. Dirt and rocks flew behind our car as the wheels dug into the earth and launched us forward.

A cloud of dirt formed behind the car ahead of us.

"He's running," James yelled, keeping the gas pedal floored. The speedometer climbed past fifty as we closed the gap.

When we got within a hundred feet. James hollered, "It's blue!" He raised his gun, aiming past me toward the vehicle.

"Put the gun down!" I yelled, ducking down in the seat.

Once he passed the car, James whipped the steering wheel hard while slamming on the brakes. I lurched forward, and we skidded sideways in front of the blue vehicle blocking the road. The blue car skidded and slammed into my side of the car. The car door crumbled, and the impact threw me against the door. Pain shot through my ribs.

James jumped out, his gun aimed at the driver.

"Where's my son?"

The driver's eyes darted wildly, panic setting in.

James ripped his door open, his face flushed, veins bulging at his neck. "Get out of the car, NOW!" he screamed, holding his gun inches from the driver's head.

The driver stumbled out, holding up his trembling hands. "Hey, man—are you crazy? Don't shoot, okay," he stammered.

I unbuckled my seatbelt, legs shaking, as I slid out the driver's side of the car. I stood, my legs still quivering like Jell-O. My belly twisted. This wasn't the same guy in my vision. I felt a wave of nausea. How in the world am I going to explain this to the police? If he pulls the trigger, would I be an accessory to murder? "James." I yelled, "Put the gun down. He's not the guy."

He didn't even glance at me, he shouted, "On the ground -- NOW!" Spittle erupted from his mouth as he screamed.

The driver dropped flat, his face buried in the dirt.

James tripped the trunk release, "If you so much as twitch, I'll kill you." James turned to me, "Check the trunk."

I dove into the trunk, throwing out a tire, carpet, some rags, a milk crate filled with tools, and a car jack. I turned to James, shaking my head. "Nothing."

James crumbled to the ground, crying, "Oh my God, he's not here." He dug his fingers into the earth, looked into the night sky, and screamed, "JOHNNY." As James pounded his fists into the earth, I heard a faint, rhythmic thump, thump, thump, emanating from the back of the vehicle.

"Wait. Something's... back here." I started searching for a latch or a grip on the back seat panel; finding it, I ripped out the panel, the plastic clips snapping with a sharp crack.

Huddled in the blackness was a small trembling body. A black hood was cinched tight around his head, his limbs hog-tied with a white rope. My heart raced as I lifted him from the cramped hold in the back seat and placed him by James on the dirt road. James, hands shaking, fumbled with the knots, finally tearing off the hood and removing the gag.

"Johnny," James choked, wrapping his arms around the boy. Johnny sobbed, "Dad!" and buried his face in James's chest.

I almost fainted with the weight of the moment. I did it. I reeled with the implications. Psychic powers were real--and I had them. My body hummed with excitement. I looked into the sky, and the stars twinkled in acknowledgment. *Trust yourself,* the words whispered into my head: *trust your visions.*

James rocked his son in his arms for a few moments. After wiping the tears from his son's face, he untied his hands. James smiled through his tears, "Your mother will never let you out of her sight again."

"I don't want her to."

James held on to his son as if Johnny would disappear at the slightest release. Johnny hugged him back with equal might. I noticed oil smeared on Johnny's blue shirt.

I touched Johnny's shirt; I felt the same oily texture of the jersey fabric.

Then I remembered the cigarette. "Is your arm okay?" I asked Johnny.

"Let me look at your arm," James said, raising Johnny's shirtsleeve. His forearm was clean, no burns.

I pulled my shirt sleeve up, my pentagon had disappeared. James and I looked at my arm and then at one another. I held out my hands, "I don't get it?" I said.

"Well, you're the psychic," James shrugged.

The driver coughed, a ragged, defiant sound.

"You know that's not the man," I told James. "I saw in my visions."

James patted my shoulder. "Hey, like you said. It's not an exact science."

"No. I have to trust my visions."

James nodded, pulled out his cell phone then keyed a number and spoke. "I have somebody here I think you want to talk to." James handed his cell phone to Johnny.

"Mom!" he yelled into the phone. Tears began streaming down the boy's cheeks. I couldn't understand a word out of that kid's mouth.

I turned to the guy spread eagle on the ground. A mark on the man's forearm peeked out from under his shirt. I said, "Hey, let me look at that mark on your arm?"

"I know who you are. Fuck you," he spat out, turning his arm around to hide it. "Call the cops; I'm innocent."

Without warning, James's leg shot out and kicked his head like he was kicking a football for a field goal. The man's head snapped to the side, his eyes rolling back for a few seconds before he groaned in pain. I was amazed that he remained conscious.

James stood over him, foot raised over his head, his voice low and dangerous. "I won't ask again."

I added, "I would do it if I were you."

The man flipped his arm over, revealing a pentagon seared into his skin- a dark, angry mark.

I gripped James's arm. "Look at that!"

"I see it," he said voice flat, eyes hard.

"He was the kid in the field."

James didn't flinch. "I don't give a shit."

I stepped back. "I'm not defending him; I'm pointing out..."

"Tie the shit bag up," James kicked the rope toward me. "I don't trust myself to do it without killing him."

I picked up the rope and tied the man's wrists behind his back. He sat there, limp and silent. When I finished, he finally spoke, "I'm free."

"What?" I asked.

"You freed me, I'm free." He stared at me with goo-goo-eyed reverence.

I frowned, "No, I just tied you up. You're concussed." I turned to James and said, "You kicked him too hard. We should call the cops."

James huffed. "They're already on their way. Did you forget they were at my house waiting with my wife?"

"So, what exactly are we telling them?"

James met my eyes, holding my gaze. "That's up to you."

I smirked, rubbing my chin. "You're right. It is up to me. And, lucky for you, I happened to be in a pretty forgiving mood," I paused, savoring the shift in control. "Almost a revelation of sorts. So, I'm willing to forgive and forget your little stunt – kidnapping me at gunpoint."

"You are?" James's face contorted, suspicion creeping into his voice. His head cocked to the side, searching for my angle.

"I am," I said casually. "I figure saving you from serving twenty years behind bars and only seeing your family occasionally through bulletproof glass is worth a little something on your end, right?"

James narrowed his eyes. "Go on."

"It's simple. Tell the truth. Tell everyone about me – papers, TV, swear to it in court. Make sure people know what I did here today."

"You're going to make money on this?" James nodded his head his lips curled into a knowing smirk, like he understood everything now.

I shrugged. "Maybe. But that's not the important thing."

"Really?" James scoffed. "What's the important thing?"

I leaned in slightly, the thought clear in my mind - *I'm not a fake.* With a smile, I said, "A door just opened for me, one that has been closed for years. So, what do you say? Do we have a deal?" I extended my hand to James.

"Deal." He muttered, gripping my hand in a firm shake.

As we released our hands, I heard the wail of police sirens approaching. A helicopter circled overhead, its blades chopping the air.

"Wow, they pulled out the big guns," I said, glancing up at the chopper.

Three police cars sped down the narrow road, the first car stopped ten feet away. The moment it halted, a woman bolted out and ran toward Johnny.

A shortish detective waddled up to me, he was a little on the round side. Pencil-thin mustache, gray hair at the temples. I felt his confidence as he stood in front of me. He swept his eyes up and down, not hiding the fact that he was sizing me up.

Behind him, a uniformed officer knelt and untied Mr. Wonderful. He grunted as the officer placed him in handcuffs and led him to the squad car.

The detective and I stood, toe to toe on the dirt road. His head was down, reading his notebook. When he finally looked up, his eyes locked on mine.

"You're Brian Miller - the psychic?"

I gave a slight nod. "I am."

I looked presentable, aside from the dried scotch stain on my shirt. I began sensing a bad vibe.

"I'm Detective Atwood out of the 119 precinct," he continued, glancing at me sharply. "So, you found Johnny Carter using your psychic powers?"

"I did," I said evenly.

"That's... amazing." He gave a skeptical chuckle. "You see I've worked lots of missing child cases. Never had a psychic lead me to one before." He glanced at his watch. "Let alone in two hours."

"Maybe a bit of luck was in play too," I offered.

"A lucky psychic. Now that's something." His eyebrows raised, mockingly intrigued. "How exactly does your psychic thing work?"

I shrugged. "It's like a game of hot and cold. I get a sense of which direction feels hotter, and I keep following it."

"Hot and cold, huh? Interesting. And that led you here?" He jotted more notes in his little booklet.

"Yes, exactly." Then, unbidden, the words publicity stunt whispered into my head, and I blurted. "This isn't a publicity stunt."

Atwood paused mid-scribble, his eyes narrowing as they rose up to meet mine. "Why would you say that, Mr. Miller?"

I shot back, "Why would you think it, Detective?"

His eyes widened just for a second, and then he recovered. "I don't believe that."

"But you did think it," I replied, smiling just enough to let him know I saw through him.

He looked me over again, more carefully this time. "I don't think anyone would risk twenty years in prison for a publicity stunt."

I nodded, keeping my expression neutral.

"Do you know Dale Oakwood, the kidnapper? He asked, changing gears."

I shook my head, "No associations."

"Ever see him anywhere, maybe in a store or a bar?"

"Never."

Atwood tucked his notebook into his jacket pocket. "I will need you to come to the police station; we need a full statement and a recount of tonight's events."

"Do I need a lawyer?" I asked.

It was the detective's turn to smile. "I don't know. You're the psychic."

I didn't realize at the moment, how many times I would hear that over the next few years.

Chapter 2 - Radio Daze

I tossed and turned in bed, trying to get comfortable. My body refused to relax. I tried Zazen breathing, focusing on the rise and fall of my chest, but my mind refused to settle.

The media frenzy for finding Johnny Carter had spiraled beyond anything I expected. Each day bought more interview requests, more attention. Even my father called to congratulate me after my interview on the Live at Five news show yesterday.

Last month, an agent reached out through my service with a contract from Caffeen Books. The advance money looked good, 200K, so, I signed and took the money. Then I learned the catch; I wouldn't see another cent until that advance was earned back through sales.

Long story short, this book has to sell. You'd think that's more of a concern for Caffeen than me, but if it tanks, so does my shot at a movie deal. Kiss that film adaptation goodbye. Yeah, the film is contingent on book sales and reviews. This book can't just be good; it needs to be stellar.

But now, I'm starting to doubt if my story will keep people hooked. Honestly, I'm not even sure if I'm psychic or a regular guy who experienced a strange psychic event. The one thing my story has going for it is that it's true.

Three months. That's all I have to deliver a finished manuscript. Caffeen hired a freelancer Terry Cott to coauthor and write my book. Who's Terry Cott? What I need is a Stephen King, not a no-name writer who's supposed to make my story sell.

This deal was not supposed to be about the money but let me tell you- it is about the money. My life is a mirage of success. I work sixty hours a week just to stay afloat- to cover my expenses; my house, car, and even that overpriced recliner in my den has a monthly payment. Sixty hours a week of grinding through the shittiest gigs across the country to keep the lights on. I'm tired of it. Tired of treading water, tired of chasing something better.

When I'm on the road, I feel like a vaudeville act. And when I can't connect with people, it becomes one. But I have my psychic routine down to a science, so those moments are rare. I know how to work the system.

For instance, if I say your mother has passed, and the client says no, my mom is still alive. Then I backpedal smoothly with; this is a female figure that's passed who's like a mother to you. It's so generic; everyone can think of someone who fits the mold.

My father said my infatuation with the paranormal wouldn't pay the bills. He was right; I've built this illusion of wealth just to prove him wrong. But for once I want him to be proud of me. And this - God damn it, is my chance. I found that boy. That was real. If I can make this book and movie deal work, I can transform my illusion into reality.

And maybe, just maybe I can finally sleep. Sweet Jesus, I just want to sleep. Instead, I'm lying here, counting breaths like it'll fix anything.

One inhale, one exhale...two inhale, two exhale.

After a few steady breaths, I heard faint static, like a radio caught between stations. I tried to ignore the sound, focusing back on the rhythm of my breaths. But every now and then an occasional word surfaced above the static, dragging my attention back to the noise. Then I strain my hearing, struggling to decipher more words.

Stop thinking about the noise. Think about sleep; about sex, about sex with Debbie.

Ours wasn't a passionate love affair that would inspire poets to write sonnets, but we had our moments. We rocked and rolled well enough.

Then the word *Emily popped* above the static, followed by the word *pottery.*

That was it! I threw the sheets off in a fit of frustration. "God damn it! If you have something to say, just say it!"

Now I'm standing in the dark yelling at unseen entities in my home. Was this another psychic event or the beginning of losing it completely?

I got up, flipped the hallway lights on, and stumbled downstairs. My den felt colder. I poured a generous portion of single malt scotch into a snifter and sank into my overpriced brown leather recliner. I sipped my scotch, savoring the rich flavor of the expensive liquor.

You may think, given my financial situation, I'd fill my expensive liquor bottle with an inexpensive blended scotch to keep up appearances. But no. First, I enjoy the taste of expensive liquor. Second, if a guest tasted the difference, poof, the illusion I built would crumble.

I set the empty glass on the side table and leaned back closing my eyes. The volume of the noise seemed lower.

Hmm, I thought. Encouraged, I poured another drink and downed it.

Nope, that didn't help.

Annoyed, I grabbed my headphones from the shelf and hit play on the Gibson player. "Wish You Were Here" by Pink Floyd started. I laughed at the irony: the song's opening is the crackle of a radio being tuned to a station, just the sound I was trying to escape. As the haunting first notes of the guitar began, the noise in my head faded. The music washed it away like waves washing away footprints in the sand.

The lyrics seeped in, loosening the tension in my shoulders. Finally, I could breathe.

I woke up at 7:00 a.m., not the best sleep, but rested enough to get by. My body groaned in protest as I reached down to pick up the headphones off the floor. Sleeping in the recliner had left me stiff, but at least it was Saturday.

I had a meeting with James Carter later that morning. I paid him $20,000 from my advance for the exclusive rights to his and his wife's side of the story. I interviewed Margaret two days ago, last Thursday, and had her story recorded and transcribed. Now it was time for James.

At 10 o'clock, I walked two blocks down into the cul-de-sac on Willowbrook Road. Young Johnny Carter was out front playing catch with three other kids under James's watchful eye.

"Hi, Johnny, who's your favorite psychic?" I called out with a grin.

"You are!" he shouted, racing over to hug me.

I handed him a small deck of cards. "These are special Zener cards. They'll help you develop your psychic abilities."

Johnny's eyes lit up. "I can become a superhero?" He jumped into the air, arms flung wide.

"Maybe." I said with a chuckle.

Margaret Carter stepped out of the house. Johnny ran over to her, waving the cards excitedly. "Hey, Mom, look what Uncle Brian gave me."

Margaret took the deck. "Did you say thank you?"

Johnny spun around. "Thank you, Uncle Brian," then darted back to his game of catch.

Margaret leaned in and kissed me on the cheek. James followed, shaking my hand.

"Storytime, right?" James asked.

I nodded, and we headed inside while Margaret stayed outside, keeping an eye on Johnny and the other kids.

* * *

I sat at the small kitchen table, its simple light wood construction offset by a yellow Formica inlay that gave it a modest charm. James rummaged through the fridge, grabbed a beer and held one out.

"Wanna beer?" he asked.

"No, I'm good, thanks." I replied.

He joined me at the table, cracking open his drink with a casual twist. "Our escapade only lasted two hours," he remarked, eyeing me with mild disbelief. "You're making that into a novel?"

I nodded. "Not a novel, a non-fiction paranormal crime story. The time frame is a bit thin; yeah, that's why I need to add your and

Margaret's perspectives. It'll fill in the gaps, flesh out the detail from outside my own experience."

James raised an eyebrow. "You want me to sit here and write my side of the story?"

"Not quite, tell me the story, and I'll record it. Pretend like you're telling the story to a buddy in a bar. Start at the beginning when you learned of Johnny's kidnapping. Don't skip over any details of what happened in the car. Even though I was there, when I channeled into the kidnapper, I didn't know what was happening around me."

Nodding, James took another sip of his beer. He set the bottle down on the table with a clink, rubbing the back of his neck. With a heavy sigh, he began, "I was at work when I received the phone call–"

"Hold up a second," I interrupted. "I need to grab my recorder."

James nodded. I quickly fetched my digital recorder from my jacket. Hitting the red record button, I placed the device between us on the table.

James cleared his throat. "It started around four o'clock; I was wrapping up some paperwork when the phone rang."

"Sorry to interrupt you again, but what type of work do you do?"

"I'm a systems analyst for the Small Business Association. Should I continue?"

"Please."

"When the phone rang at work, I saw Margaret's name on the caller ID. When I answered, she was crying hysterically. I couldn't make sense of it at first, but eventually I pieced together that Johnny had been abducted near his school." James paused, his voice steady but strained. "I left work immediately. When I pulled into our parking lot, there were two police vehicles outside. My neighbors were gathered in small groups, talking quietly. I remember hoping - praying - that maybe the cops had found Johnny and brought him home."

He exhaled slowly, shaking his head, the weight of the memory still fresh. "When I walked inside, Margaret ran over to me, and threw herself into my arms. I tried to comfort her, but there was nothing I could say or do to help."

"I understand," I said.

"A neighbor gave her Valium to calm her down, but it had no effect. You remember Detective Atwood?" James asked, his tone shifting.

I nodded. "I do."

James's voice grew hard. "He questioned me; asking all stupid shit – did I have any enemies? Was I seeing someone on the side? Anyone out there who might want to hurt us? I told him no to all of it, I had no enemies or girlfriend, --no one I knew who would want to hurt us. The clock kept ticking. When you're just sitting there waiting for news, it messes with your head. Margaret was falling apart, getting more desperate by the minute. I took a few Valiums with a shot of whiskey just to steady my nerves."

I must've made a face that reflected my thoughts that he held a gun to my head while in a drugged state, because James gave me a wary look, "Hey, I'm not getting myself into a legal situation by telling you all this, am I?"

"No, not at all." I assured him. "I'll leave out the part about the pills - along with using the gun to motivate me into finding your son; that's not going into the story. Do you have coffee?"

James nodded, got up to brew a pot. A few minutes later, he placed a steaming cup in front of me, then sat down and continued. "After a while, I walked upstairs to my bedroom just to be alone for a moment. Margaret followed me. She dropped to her knees, grabbed my legs, and begged me – begged me - to find Johnny. Do whatever you need to do, she says, but bring my boy back home." His voice cracked slightly, James shook his head as if to clear the memory.

He hesitated, "Should I mention the gun or leave it out?"

"Put it in; the gun is essential near the end. Like I said, I'll edit out that you used it to coerce me."

James raised an eyebrow, smirking slightly. "I have to say, you're taking me putting a gun to your head quite well. You're here, and we're chatting like old friends."

I took a deep breath and let it out slowly. Do I tell him the crisis he created woke up my psychic powers? No, there is no benefit to me for him to know that. "I am looking at the bigger picture, and that perspective seems to be a better one to have."

James nodded his acceptance of my answer. "After Margaret begged me, I told her I would search the neighborhood, starting at the school. I went into my nightstand and pulled out my nine-millimeter, threw it in a small duffle bag and walked right past the police to my car. I started driving to the school, but as I passed your house, I remembered my wife telling me about one of your psychic events she attended. That's when I got the idea to engage your services."

I laughed, "*Engage my services?* Cute. Like someone running Jack the Ripper's dating service." James smiled, holding up the coffee pot. "More coffee?"

* * *

After returning home, I played back the recording and jotted down notes for Monday. James's perspective added some much-needed depth, and I managed to outline the first five chapters. When my brain could not handle any more, I grabbed Dean Koontz's *Odd Thomas* and settled into bed, reading until I caught myself nodding off.

The moment I rested my head on the pillow, the radio static started again. The name Emily became audible above the noise. New words I couldn't recognize kept repeating. I listened until I was tired of listening.

Why is everything psychic so difficult? I thought bitterly.

Stumbling into my den, I poured myself a scotch, filling the small snifter and draining it in one go. I grabbed my headphones, collapsed into the recliner, and hit the play button. Pink Floyd's "Shine On You Crazy Diamond" filled my ears, burying the maddening static. The last thing I remember is hearing the chorus.

* * *

Monday morning, Terry arrived promptly at 10:30, carrying a tan leather messenger bag that looked ready to burst at the seams. Her dark brown hair, streaked with blonde highlights, caressed her shoulders. Intense hazel eyes peered out from behind thick, black horn-rimmed glasses, and her pointed chin added sharpness to her soft features. Dressed in a thin white blouse and tan slacks, she was both stylish and professional. I guessed her to be in her early 30s

Standing in the doorway, she smiled and extended her hand. "Hi, I'm Terry Cott."

The moment our hands touched, an unexpected image flashed in my mind: a tall man draped in a white sheet, pretending to be a ghost, yelling, *Boo*. Startled, I pulled my hand back. *Wow! This is new*, I thought.

Terry tilted her head, confused. "What?"

"Nothing," I said, brushing it aside. Prepared, I took her hand, and like magic, the image reappeared. *Boo*, the ghost repeated and laughed, throwing off the white sheet to reveal a young man with red hair and a thick beard standing confidently on the ledge of a mountain. His right hand rested on his chest; his left gave the okay sign.

I squinted, raising my hand to my brow to focus on the image, "I see a tall man with red hair and a beard. He has pulled a white sheet over himself, holding his arms up, pretending to be a ghost, and yelling, Boo!"

Terry's eyes widened. "That's Tommy, my brother!"

"So this makes sense to you?" I asked, slightly surprised.

She nodded, a soft smile tugging at her lips. "He always said if he died first, he'd come back as a ghost to scare me."

I glanced at her hair. "He has red hair, and you're a brunette."

"Genetics," She explained with a shrug.

"Why the mountain?"

"He loved climbing." She wiped tears away. "Is he okay?"

I shrugged. "He seemed happy and laughing."

"Try again," she asked, holding out her hand.

I reached out and touched her hand again. Nothing. "He didn't come back. Sorry."

Terry studied me with that mischievous smile still playing on her lips. "So, you *are* for real?"

I let out a long exhale. "Apparently. I wish people would stop asking me that. But tell me - why are you writing my book if you don't think the material's real?"

Her smile widened. "Hey, it's a fat paycheck. But I'll write the shit out of your story if you're really legit."

"Please do," I said, gesturing down the hallway to my office.

* * *

Once inside, I sat behind my desk, while Terry wandered over to admire the oil painting of deep space by Dave Archer that hung on the wall.

"Nice." She commented, before crossing the room and taking a seat in the leather chair opposite me.

"I've been thinking about the structure of the book," I began. "We should open with a bit of my personal history, how I got into providing psychic readings," I said. "Then we bring in Margaret and James's story of Johnny being abducted. After that, we dive into the main event, where I got involved. As you write forward from this point, I think it would be compelling if you intertwined James's perspective with mine. I think it would add layers to the story."

Terry nodded thoughtfully. "Yeah, dual perspective could really amp up the tension. It'll give readers a fuller view of what was happening at every moment, especially when you channeled into the kidnapper."

"Exactly," I said, leaning back in my chair. "The more angles we show, the more real it'll feel."

"Sounds workable, I'll try it," she agreed, pulling some papers from her bag. "I made copies of the police report and dug up background information on Dale Oakwood." She handed me the stack. "Oakwood had a rough childhood-- alcoholic mom, abusive father, and get this, his dad pimped him out as a kid. Real prince of a guy. When Mom found out, they divorced. He later got into satanic worship in his twenties, which ties in nicely with your psychic visions of him. He made a killing in real estate until the market crashed. After that, he lost everything and started spiraling and was prone to violent outbursts, especially against women."

"How did you get all this?" I asked, skimming the papers.

"I called his friends, associates, and even his parents. Turns out they are still alive and willing to talk. I told them I was working for a local publication, doing an article about the upcoming trial. They opened right up."

We spent the next two and a half hours diving deeper into the story, hammering out critical details and refining the structure. I handed Terry copies of all my notes, and the five chapters I outlined. She took her own notes in a spiral notebook—then jotted down even more notes about my notes.

By the end, it felt like the pieces were finally coming together.

"We'll end the book with the happy reunion between father and son, Terry said, her voice confident, "and the epilogue will be the results of the criminal trial scheduled in March. I'll come back as soon as I've finished fleshing out the first five chapters.

"Sounds good. Want a drink?"

She smiled politely, tucking her notebook into her messenger bag. "Too early for me, thanks."

I glanced at my watch—almost one o'clock. "What about lunch then? I know a nice spot on the island."

Terry hesitated for a moment before giving me a firm look. "Brian, our relationship needs to stay professional. Nothing personal can get in the way of us working together to produce the best book possible."

I shrugged, masking my disappointment. "Sure."

She smirked, pulling a red scrunchie from her bag and tying her hair into a ponytail, a few strands falling loose around her face. "I could tell you I have a boyfriend, but with what you can do ..." Her tone was teasing, but there was curiosity in her eyes.

"Mind reading?" I asked with a raised eyebrow.

"Can you?"

I shook my head. "I never want to work that hard."

"So, it's not a trick?"

Terry was sharp, attractive, and clearly trying to figure out how deep my abilities really went. I glanced at her for a moment, weighing my words. Wanting to build a little rapport, I said, "It's easier to guide someone's thoughts than to read them. That takes practice."

Her lips curled into a mischievous smile. "So, mind reading isn't real?"

"It's both real and not, depending on the situation. Always difficult," I replied, keeping things just ambiguous enough.

"Since I'm not psychic, tell me the trick?" Her eyes lit up like a child's.

I smiled, leaning back. "First, you must get the person to think about what you're trying to read. If you're trying to guess a number but they're thinking about what's for dinner tonight, you are out of luck. The hardest bit, though, is making your mind still and fully focused on the person. You have to stay in this state, so you are receptive to impressions from their mind."

Terry tilted her head, unconvinced. "That doesn't sound very hard to do."

"Alright, let's try a quick experiment," I said, glancing at the wall clock. "For 30 seconds, think of anything you want—just don't think of yellow jellybeans. Anything else is fair game, but no yellow jellybeans. Ready?" I watched the secondhand move. "Go."

Ten seconds passed. Twenty seconds.

Terry broke into laughter. "I can't! All I can think about is yellow jellybeans!"

"Exactly," I said. "Okay, now let's flip it. Think all you want about yellow jellybeans, but for the next 30 seconds, don't think of red jellybeans. Don't let red jellybeans enter your mind at all. Ready? Set, go."

Ten seconds went by before she sighed, giving up.

"You win," Terry said, grinning. "It's impossible."

"And that's the point," I replied with a smirk. "It's not easy to control what you focus on—or what others focus on."

"The key to mind reading is discipline," I continued. "You have to make your mind as still as water. Hold that stillness and stay focused on the person until you start to get impressions, like little ripples coming from their mind."

Terry laughed. "Now, it sounds hard."

I shrugged. "Everyone is capable. It just takes practice."

"Oh no, not me," she said with a cheerful grin. "Too much work."

I nodded. "It's not a casual thing."

"Good." She replied, smiling. "In that case... I have a boyfriend."

"Thank God! For a moment, I thought I needed to sleep with you."

Her expression shifted, a quick flash of bewilderment crossing her face.

"You said you have a boyfriend," I explained. "So, there's no reason for me to sleep with you, for you to write the shit out of my story, right?"

Terry squinted, then returned my smile. "Right. None at all. Give me a week to flesh out the chapters, and I'll come back so we can review them together."

"Why not email them?"

"I prefer face-to-face discussions with my authors. Less chance of misinterpretation. The subtleties of writing are hard to convey in an email." She extended her hand for a handshake.

"Okay," I said, taking her hand. I paused a second; her skin was warm, and something tugged at the edge of my awareness. "You're missing something in your life, aren't you?"

"Aren't we all?" she said lightly, but I sensed something deeper.

"No," I replied, more confidently. "It's intimacy, I think."

She laughed, though her smile faltered. "Ha! Trying to play me now?"

I shook my head. "No, I see an emotionally unavailable man. Is that what's missing?"

Her reaction was immediate—she jerked her hand away from mine. "You told me you couldn't read minds."

"I'm not reading your mind," I replied, feigning indignation. "I'm sensing your feelings."

"Bull." She brushed past me and opened the front door, clearly irritated.

With her back to me, I heard her say loudly, "Keep trying, old man!"

What? I froze for a second. *Old man?* Sure, I might be a few years older, but I was not an old man. And I wasn't going to be spoken to like that in my own home.

"Old man?" I repeated, the disbelief evident in my voice. "Keep trying? I'm not trying, least of all for you!"

Terry spun around, her face draining of color. Her hand shot up to cover her mouth, eyes wide with shock. "You said you couldn't read minds."

My heart pounded. I threw my hands up in frustration. "Forget it! Just pretend I'm some old fraud who made a lucky guess."

"Shit! I'm sorry," she stammered, shaking her head. "I was thinking that, I would never have said it out loud."

I felt my face flush. "You were leaving, so leave."

Terry rushed out, shutting the door behind her. The moment it clicked, a surge of excitement ran through me – I could barely contain it. I hopped up and down, clapping my hands like a kid. My psychic powers were growing. My elation was short-lived as static howled in my ears, loud and piercing.

"What do you want?" I yelled into the empty room, and the howling subsided.

* * *

I wandered into the kitchen and made a turkey and American cheese sandwich. Sitting at the table, I took a bite and chewed slowly, thinking. *Maybe I should've been a bigger person and handled it differently. Perhaps it's my age. Nah, rejection stings at any age. But the look on her face when she realized I'd heard her thoughts - oh my God, priceless!*

Squeaks, my elusive cat, chose that moment to make an appearance after being gone for two days. She rubbed against the bottom of my legs, purring.

"Hungry, are we?" I said, opening a can of food. She began eating as soon as the dish hit the floor.

It was only 2:00, but I was beyond exhausted. As soon as I lay on the bed to nap, the static returned. Words floated above the noise; "Emily" always cut through. I dragged myself out of bed and went to my den. I poured myself a drink, cued Pink Floyd, and put on my headphones.

I must've fallen out because I was jolted awake when the doorbell chimed. Groggy, I checked the time -- 3:30 pm. I shuffled to the front door, still in a daze.

Standing there was a woman in her mid-30s, with a heart-shaped face and minimal makeup, just a hint of eyeliner accentuating her amber eyes. Her light brown hair framed her porcelain skin. She was impeccably dressed, holding a Louis Vuitton bag and wearing Jimmy Choo shoes. A sleek white Mercedes was parked in front of my house.

"Mr. Brian Miller?" she inquired, her voice calm but laced with tension.

"Yes?" I replied, still shaking off the grogginess.

She glanced over her shoulder, then back to me. "My name is Emily Potts. I have a paranormal issue, and I'm hoping you can help me."

Emily! The name hit me like a tsunami, but I forced myself to remain calm. "Please, come in," I said, opening the door wider, "Let's see what we can do."

I led her into the living room, where she sat on the couch. I took the oak chair across from her, sensing her nervous energy.

"So?" I prompted.

"I believe my house is haunted," she said, hesitating as if unsure how to continue. She shook her left foot on the floor nervously.

I rubbed my chin, leaning forward. "Why do you say that?"

She bit her lip, clearly embarrassed. "I hear a baby crying at night. At first, I thought it was my daughter, Anna, but every time I checked, she was always fast asleep. I can tell the crying is somewhere in my house. When I try to track it, the crying moves. It's like it's toying with me. My hair stands on end when I hear it."

"Has anyone else heard this -- like a partner?"

"No partner, I'm a single mom," she said. "Anna's father is a musician. He wasn't ready to be a dad, so we agreed it was better for him to stay out of her life. I mean, that's better than him coming in and out sporadically." Emily shook her leg nervously. "Would you mind if I smoke? Normally, I wouldn't ask, but I noticed the ashtrays."

I nodded. "Go ahead. I'm a former smoker myself -- I enjoy secondhand smoke."

Emily opened her handbag and pulled out a pack of Parliament cigarettes, lighting one and taking a slow drag.

"You believe me?" she asked, her voice quieter now, uncertain.

"Of course," I said, handing her the sand-bottomed ashtray. "Why else would you be here?"

"Thank you," Emily said, exhaling a plume of smoke. "I was afraid to tell anyone lest they think I'm losing it. I'm a producer for cable TV, and I can't have people questioning my sanity."

"I understand." I took in the second-hand smoke. "How long have you lived in the house?"

"About two months. The crying started after I brought Anna home from the hospital, so about a month ago. The house itself is about 40 years old, and as far as I know, no bad history."

"Anyone else live in the house?"

"No, just me. During the day, I have my babysitter, Cathy. But she hadn't heard anything. It only happens at night."

"When you're alone?" I pressed.

Emily nodded, looking uneasy. *Things that go bump in the night.* I thought. "I guess I'll need to spend the night to investigate."

"That's not a problem, Anna and I are staying at the Hilton Hotel on South Ave, by the Teleport." She crushed her cigarette out in the ashtray. "When can you spend the night?"

"Tonight works," I said, leaning back.

Her eyes flickered with relief. "What do you charge for your services?"

"For a standard consultation, I charge $500. Since this involves an overnight stay, it'll be $1,000. But I'll keep my fees capped regardless of how long this takes," I said. Thinking - *I need the experience as much as the money.*

"That is acceptable." She hesitated before adding, "I can't have this get out, like the Johnny Carter case. I need your discretion."

"I am discrete," I assured her. "If I decide to write about your case, it will remain anonymous."

Emily exhaled, a mix of frustration and hope in her voice. "Do you really think you can help?"

"Yes," I said, nodding. "It feels like a calling." I glanced around, half expecting to hear static kick in, but there was only silence.

* * *

Emily and I agreed that I'd arrive at her home around 5 pm.

Her house was tucked away from street view, hidden behind a thick fence of bushes and trees, with a hundred-foot driveway leading to the front. I followed the inlaid stone path to the door, where a two-story Tudor stood proudly on a well-manicured lawn. Two white columns flanked the entrance, supporting an overhanging roof above the entrance. The double doors were adorned with circular glass windows, each etched with a delicate Celtic knot.

I pressed the embossed doorbell, hearing a soft chime from within. A minute later, Emily opened the door and wordlessly led me through a spacious hallway to what could have been a page ripped from an architectural magazine. The living room, a step down from the main hall, was blanketed in a plush white carpet, with a luxurious white leather couch at its center. To the left was an entrance to a library, where ceiling-high bookshelves framed a fireplace. Leather recliners and small glass tables were arranged neatly around it. To the right, double glass doors led into an atrium bursting with potted plants, bathed in the soft glow of natural light from milky white translucent roof panels.

It was a lot to take in—a house full of elegance and precision.

I'm a pauper. I thought. *This is the difference between pretending to be wealthy and actually being so.*

An older white-haired woman sat on the couch, cradling the baby in her arms. Her faded blue eyes looked up as Emily introduced us.

"Cathy, let me introduce you to Brian Miller, our paranormal investigator," Emily said.

The woman sized me up with a curious gaze. "You're the ghost hunter?" she asked, her voice carried the skepticism of someone who had seen a lot and believed very little.

"I am," I replied, stepping closer to Cathy, who was gently playing with baby Anna. As I moved, something strange pulled at my senses. It felt as if the baby was the center of gravity, pulling everything into her orbit. I leaned in to get a better look at her face.

Suddenly, a woman's voice shrieked, "Stop!"

Cathy flinched, and I jerked back instinctively. Baby Anna began crying.

I spun toward Emily, my heart racing. "You heard that?" I asked.

Emily looked startled but nodded her head. "Something fell in the kitchen." She hurried through a swinging door behind us, leaving me with Cathy.

Cathy rocked the baby in her arms, feeding her a bottle, her voice low and uneasy. "Things are not right in this house."

"What's not right? What have you experienced?"

She hesitated, her eyes never leaving the baby's face. "Things falling, I saw a glass of water sliding off a table by itself and shattering on the floor."

Just then, Emily returned, holding a large copper cooking pot. "This fell to the floor. I don't know how - it was hanging on a two-inch hook. These are the things that keep happening."

Cathy's eyes darted nervously about the room, checking corners.

"You didn't hear a woman scream?" I asked.

Emily shook her head. "No, just the pot crashing to the floor in the kitchen."

"Me, too," Cathy agreed. "No scream, just the pot." She handed Anna over to Emily. "I think I'd better get going; it's getting late."

"Okay, be careful getting home," Emily said.

"You be careful too. Things are not right in this house," she repeated.

As Cathy hurried out the door, Emily turned to me. "Now you know why I can't stay here."

"You mentioned hearing a baby crying in the night, not objects being thrown around."

"It escalated," she admitted, glancing away. "I didn't mention it because I didn't want you to think me crazy."

"I don't think you're crazy at all," I reassured her.

"Should I stay with you or go to the hotel?"

"Go to the hotel. I'll call if anything happens."

"I'll be back around 7 in the morning, Cathy's in at 7:30, and I leave at 8 for work."

"Okay, that's fine," I said, rubbing my chin. As I spoke, a wave of unease swept through me, a feeling in the pit of my stomach like the feeling you get at the top of a roller coaster just before the drop, like that, only worse. Clutching Anna, Emily hurried out.

The instant the door closed behind her, the temperature plummeted. It was like stepping inside a freezer. Icy wind blasted my face, raising goosebumps. I could see my breath cloud in the freezing air as I exhaled. The atmosphere crackled with static that stood the hairs on my arms straight up. My heart raced. I tensed up, preparing for something closing in.

I wasn't ready.

The air whipped around me like a living creature, twisting and writhing. It slithered beneath my clothes, biting into my skin with icy tendrils. Thin lines of white frost swirled around me like ghostly fingers. I tried to move, to leave, but my feet were stuck - frozen to the floor. I couldn't lift them. I couldn't run.

The atmosphere crackled louder, buzzing in my ears. Flashes of light sparked in the corners of my eyes like tiny bolts of lightning. I forced my foot forward, inch by painful inch. Every step felt like wading through concrete, my muscles screaming in protest. Each movement was a battle, my legs burning with the effort.

I pushed again, shifting my other foot, but the air fought back. It roared in my ears, swirling more violently as if the house was trying to keep me there.

Five feet from the door, I gasped for air, each breath like fire in my lungs. The weight of the air pressed down on me, thick and unrelenting, but I forced myself forward. When I finally reached the door, my hands shook as I grasped the knob. I needed both hands to turn it. I pulled on the door, but it wouldn't budge. I braced my foot against the jamb, pulling harder, but the door stayed wedged.

God damn it. I hissed; the muscles in my back and arms burned as I strained against the force holding the door shut.

Slowly, agonizingly, the door crept open. I kept pulling, my muscles screaming with the effort. When I wrenched the door clear of the jam by a foot, I twisted my body and flung myself through the gap. I fell hard onto the pavement outside.

I lay there, feeling the warm pavement against my cheek; my chest heaving, my breath coming in hard gasps, my heart pounding in my ears.

Looking down the driveway, I saw Emily packing her stroller into the trunk of her car. She stopped mid-motion and turned to me. I blinked, disoriented. I thought she had left; it felt like I had been fighting my way out of the house for an hour.

"Brian!" She called, rushing up the walkway, high heels clicking against the inlaid stones. "Oh my God, what happened to you? Are you okay?"

She held Anna in one arm and reached down with the other, but I waved her hand away, forcing myself to stand on trembling legs. My knees buckled for a second, but I straightened myself and stood.

When I met her gaze, Emily froze, eyes wide with horror. She took a step back.

"What happened?" she whispered, "Did you see a ghost? Your face is white... your lips are purple." She reached out and touched my hand. "My God, you're as cold as ice."

I rubbed my hands together, attempting to generate some warmth. Then I cupped them around my mouth, blowing to get them warm.

"What happened in there?" Emily asked urgently.

"Nothing to speak of," I lied, trying to regain my composure.

"Nothing?" Her voice rose, incredulous. "I was only out here for a minute. It looks like nothing almost killed you."

"I wasn't prepared," I admitted, still rubbing my hands together, trying to shake off the lingering cold. "I got overwhelmed. I need to come back tomorrow night if that's okay with you."

Emily shook her head firmly, her eyes narrowing. "No. Brian, this looks way beyond you. I can't let you go back in there, not after this. I don't want to be responsible if you get hurt—or worse."

"Please, Emily." I touched her arm gently, my voice steady despite the tremor running through me. "Give me another chance. I know what I'm doing. This is my calling."

She folded her arms across her chest, frowning deeply. "Look at yourself. What happens next time? What if it gets worse?" she asked, her voice tight with worry.

"I told you, I wasn't prepared," I repeated, searching for the right words. "I went in expecting a lighter presence—like a child's spirit. But whatever is in that house... It's not a baby, Emily."

She stared at me, unsure, her skepticism evident. I opened my mouth to continue, but a word whispered through my mind, unbidden: *Guardian.*

Without thinking, I repeated it aloud. "Guardian?"

Emily's brow furrowed. "What? What do you mean, *Guardian?* Is that what's in the house?"

"I don't know." I paused, my mind racing to catch up with my own words. "It's... an impression. That's why I need to come back. There's more at play here than just a restless spirit. I need to figure out what—or *who*—we're dealing with."

Emily bit her lip, uncertainty flashing across her face. "You're saying there's something else in there?"

I nodded slowly. "Maybe. But until I go back, I can't say for sure. All I know is that this thing—it's powerful, and it's not going to let go easily."

These things are real, I thought, rubbing the back of my neck. *Things do go bump in the night. This wasn't some carnival trick, no smoke and mirrors, no hocus pocus. A genuine, no-bullshit, paranormal event. This is some serious shit. There is more to the universe than meets the eye, and now I'm in the middle of it.*

Emily asked again, "Are you sure you can do this?"

"I can," I declared, trying to sound steady. "And I will." The words came with more confidence than I felt, a confidence I hoped would still be with me when I went back inside that house.

The next day, I found myself on Mulberry Street in lower Manhattan, inside a small spy shop crammed with surveillance gear. I picked up several low-light wireless mini-cams and a DVR to capture all the footage. If something happened—and I was certain it would—it wouldn't just be my word this time. I needed proof, something concrete.

But there was one more thing I needed, something I didn't want to admit I was considering.

I dialed James and arranged a meeting.

* * *

The cul-de-sac on Seneca Loop was becoming too familiar, like a place I wished I could avoid but couldn't.

James opened the door, his face set in a puzzled frown. "I sent Margaret and Johnny out shopping. What's so urgent?"

I took a breath, feeling the weight of the ask, "I need to borrow your gun."

The silence that followed was thick, hanging in the air between us.

James stared at me, his brow knitting together as he stood aside, motioning me in. We walked into the kitchen, the tension palpable.

"Why?"

"Protection," I said flatly. "I'm spending the night in a haunted house."

James smirked, shaking his head. "Ghosts are already dead, man. A gun's not gonna help you there."

"What if it's not a ghost?"

His smirk faded. He shrugged, crossing his arms. "Even so, I can't just lend you my gun. It's illegal. If you hurt someone, I'm on the hook."

"I get that," I said, meeting his eyes. "But what if I *stole* your gun? Without you technically knowing, you're not liable for anything. It's only for emergencies. I swear I won't hurt anyone." I tapped the envelope stuffed with cash. "Five thousand dollars for three days."

James's eyebrows shot up. "Five grand?"

I nodded, watching him closely as he ran through the numbers in his head.

"You're not... gunning for revenge, right? This isn't some payback thing?"

I shook my head. "No. It's a real haunted house, and I don't know what's in there, but it's not friendly."

"You're serious?" His voice softened, like he was half-expecting me to crack a grin.

"As a heart attack."

James leaned back, the skepticism creeping back into his expression. "Well, I've got some silver bullets, made special for me, extra hundred if you want those too?"

"Yes, absolutely," I replied, dead serious.

James bent over, laughing. "You honestly think I have silver bullets for hunting werewolves."

I wasn't amused. "You offered." I crossed my arms, watching him laugh, but soon, despite myself, I found myself chuckling. "You're a jerk."

We both laughed, and the tension broke.

* * *

James kept his gun in his nightstand by the bed. While I finished up in the adjacent bathroom, I could hear him walking downstairs, his footsteps fading as he left me alone.

I stepped into his bedroom, my pulse quickening as I opened the nightstand drawer. The gun lay there, cool and still, a tangible weight in my hands. I slipped it into my briefcase and closed it quietly.

Downstairs, we stood in the kitchen. James glanced at the briefcase, but his expression remained neutral. It felt like Schrödinger's experiment—his gun was both there and not, if he didn't check the drawer. For the next three days, he'd be living in that uncertainty.

"Thanks for letting me use the bathroom," I said, keeping my tone casual as I placed the envelope on the kitchen table—fifty crisp hundred-dollar bills stacked inside.

James gave a nod, his eyes flicking to the money. He didn't say a word, and I wasn't sure if it was relief or suspicion tightening his jaw.

With that, I grabbed my briefcase and headed for the door.

"Three days," James said.

"Three days, " I replied, walking out without looking back.

* * *

* * *

I unlocked the front door to Emily's house, the house was eerily quiet, and as I stepped inside, I half-expected the air to turn icy, charged with the strange energy I'd felt the day before. But the air was still and unnervingly normal.

I set my Pelican case down by the glass coffee table, my briefcase resting on the couch beside it. For a moment, I stood there, waiting—waiting for that cold, electric surge that should have greeted me. Nothing. Just silence.

With a sigh, I unpacked the wireless cameras and DVR, setting them up in every key spot, exactly as the surveillance expert had instructed. The cameras covered the living room, kitchen, hallway—any area where something could slip by unseen. If anything came for me while I slept, it wouldn't escape the lenses.

After checking the connections, I sat down on the couch and pulled the gun from my briefcase. The cold metal felt foreign in my hands. I stared at it for a long moment, debating whether to keep the safety on or off. My thumb hesitated over the safety before I clicked it on, leaving the gun resting on my lap.

I leaned back, letting out a breath I didn't realize I'd been holding, and closed my eyes. I strained to hear it—that static, the strange signal from the other night—but the house remained quiet.

As sleep crept up on me, the tension in my shoulders eased. I drifted off.

When I woke, a glance at my watch told me it was 11:45 pm. I'd been out for nearly two hours. Rubbing the sleep from my eyes, I checked the DVR, rewinding the footage at 10x speed.

Nothing.

I stood up, stretching the stiffness from my muscles, and made my way to the kitchen. The house still felt strangely mundane—nothing like the haunted fortress I had fought my way out of the previous night.

"Hey!" I called out into the quiet, my voice sounding almost too loud. "You called me, remember?"

Silence answered back.

I opened the fridge, grabbed the orange juice, and poured myself a glass. The normalcy of it all—opening a fridge, drinking juice—felt surreal in this place where I knew something wasn't right. I wasn't here for a midnight snack. I was here to face whatever the hell was lurking in this house. And it was making me wait.

I woke to the soft sound of footsteps and the faint rustle of a bag. Blinking against the morning light, I saw Emily moving through the living room.

"Come into the kitchen," she said over her shoulder, barely slowing her pace. "I brought coffee and bagels."

I pushed myself off the couch, the stiffness from the night spent there pulling at my muscles. The house felt eerily normal in the daylight; it was quiet, almost mocking. I followed Emily into the kitchen.

"Coffee smells good," I said, grateful for something to shake off the grogginess.

"Dunkin's the best," she said with a small smile, handing me a paper cup. The heat felt comforting in my hands.

"Where's Anna?" I asked after taking a sip.

"Cathy's watching her at the Hilton today," Emily replied, her tone tight. "Last night freaked her out, so she needed a break."

"I see," I said, nodding. There was an undercurrent to Emily's words, but I didn't push.

She paused, eyeing me over her coffee cup. "Did anything happen last night?"

I shook my head. "Nothing. No impressions, no visitations—nothing." I stretched my arms above my head, feeling the tension in my spine ease a little. "The couch was more comfortable than I expected, though."

Emily set the bagels on the table, frustration flickering in her eyes. "I don't get it. Why would it attack you one day and leave you alone the next?"

She moved around the kitchen with quiet efficiency, pulling the bagels from the paper bag. I could feel her anxiety simmering.

"I've been thinking about that all night," I said, sliding into a chair. "What I'm starting to believe is that whatever's here wants you and the baby. It's tied to you, to something unresolved. It only got angry when I suggested you leave the house."

Emily's hand faltered as she set the bagels on the table. Her face tightened, a flicker of dread passing over her features.

I leaned forward, my voice steady but firm. "If I'm right, we need to try again. But this time, you and Anna have to be here."

She nodded slowly, her eyes distant as she processed what I was saying. "Yeah... I was afraid that might be the case."

The weight of the needed action hung between us. I understood she didn't want to bring Anna back into the house, but she understood—whatever was haunting them wasn't done with them yet.

* * *

I returned at 8:00 p.m., and the moment I crossed the threshold, the air was charged again—crackling with strange electricity that seemed to hum just beneath the surface. It felt alive.

From the living room, I could hear Emily's soft voice as she dressed Anna for bed, playing peek-a-boo. The baby's laughter rang out, innocent and pure, cutting through the charged atmosphere. As Emily tugged on Anna's onesie, pulling the fabric over her tiny arms, I could feel the air around me swirl, like invisible hands brushing against my skin.

Showtime, I thought.

Emily sat down on the couch, cradling Anna in her arms. She undid the top three buttons of her blouse. "I'm going to nurse. Do you mind?"

"No." I turned away, giving her privacy, and checked the camera feeds connected to the DVR. Everything was live, recording. The hairs on my arms stood on end again, that strange static buzzing in the back of my mind. Something was coming.

Emily's voice wavered behind me. "I hear a baby crying. Do you hear it?"

I paused, listening intently, but heard nothing. "No," I replied, keeping my voice steady. But I could feel it—a pressure in the air. Instead of relying on just my hearing, I opened up, using my whole body like an antenna, trying to feel rather than listen.

A strange sensation crept over me, like being caught in a slow, gentle current. I swayed, side to side, as if submerged in water, caught in the swells of the ocean, my body moving without my control.

"You don't hear it?" Emily's voice rose, tinged with fear.

"No," I repeated, but my own voice sounded distant. The swaying intensified, the unseen force pulling at me, making it impossible to keep my balance. I stumbled, then dropped to my knees, the world tilting around me.

"Brian, what's wrong?" Emily's voice was sharp now, panic setting in.

"I'm okay, just dizzy," I mumbled, my cheek pressed against the carpet. The coarse fibers scratched at my skin, grounding me for a moment, but the sensation of swaying—of being on a boat in rough seas—grew worse. My vision blurred, the room spinning around me. The air was thick with energy, swirling, pressing down on me.

I took a deep breath, exhaled slowly, and closed my eyes again. The sensations intensified, my sense of up and down dissolving into disorienting nothingness. Static howled in my ears, like a radio tuned to chaos. Above the din, a faint voice broke through: "Mother... mommy..."

Instinctively, I repeated the impression aloud, feeling the words form almost involuntarily. "Mother... mommy. Does that make any sense to you?" My voice wavered as the swaying sensation became more violent. I kept my eyes shut, the dizziness making me sick. Another whisper rose above the noise, clearer this time.

"My sister."

The words burst out of me, sharp and unfiltered. Suddenly, images began flashing in my mind, quick and jarring. I saw a coffin—small, tiny, heartbreakingly so. "I see a coffin," I murmured, struggling to steady myself. "It's tiny. A baby's coffin."

The picture sharpened, becoming clearer. "A baby... in a crib. Cold. Not moving. It's dead." The finality of the words hit me like a blow, the image freezing in my mind.

Somewhere in the distance, I heard Emily sobbing softly, but I couldn't pull myself out of the vision. The scene shifted, warped, and suddenly there were flowers—but no, not flowers. One flower. A rose.

I see a rose, I said. The word **remember** bubbled up through the static, and I shouted it without thinking. "Remember!" The room spun violently, and I felt the floor flip beneath me. My stomach heaved, and I vomited, the sensation overwhelming.

Gradually, the swaying stopped. The room steadied itself, the oppressive force easing off. I raised myself onto my hands and knees, gasping for breath. My shirt clung to my skin, soaked with sweat, and my throat burned from the bile. For a long moment, I stayed there, the room spinning in slow motion around me.

When I looked up, Emily was staring at me, tears streaming down her face. She cradled Anna in her arms, still nursing, but her expression was filled with raw emotion, her body trembling.

"Tell me," I rasped, my voice rough.

Emily's voice cracked as she spoke. "My first daughter... Rose... she died in her crib." She paused, swallowing back a sob. "The doctors said it was SIDS."

I stared at her, the weight of her words sinking in. "So... this is Rose?"

Emily nodded, tears spilling freely now. "I tried to forget her," she whispered, her voice breaking. "When she died, I didn't know if I could go on. I didn't want to *remember.*"

Now there was something else—an underlying presence that had been waiting. A low, chilling voice cut through the quiet, like the rasp of dead leaves in the wind. I felt it, "*Rose is not alone.*"

I froze, closing my eyes, and a dark figure formed in my mind. A woman—ancient, with a face etched in pain and fury. Her eyes were black voids, hollow yet piercing, and she was cradling something in her arms. Her child.

"Who... are you?" I whispered, my voice barely audible.

"*I am her mother.*" The voice was sharp, cold. "*She is mine. I protect her.*"

A surge of cold shot through me, more powerful than anything I'd felt before. This was an old spirit tied to this land.

"Emily," I croaked, barely able to find my voice. "There's... another spirit. A woman. She's—she's been here a long time."

Emily's eyes widened, her tears freezing in place. "What are you talking about?"

"She's protecting Rose. A woman, centuries old.

Emily's face went pale, the color draining from her cheeks. "Oh my God..." she whispered. "What do we do?"

Brian stood in the center of the living room, the air crackling with static from unseen forces. His breath fogged in front of him. Somewhere in the distance, Emily gently rocked Anna, trying to keep the child calm.

He felt her—Esmeralda. The ancient spirit's swirled through the room like a cold wind, carrying centuries of anguish, protectiveness, and fury. She had spent lifetimes bound to this land, where her home once stood, convinced she had found her lost child in Rose. Esmeralda had wrapped herself around Rose's spirit, believing she was protecting her from the cruel world that had taken everything from her.

As Esmeralda's strength gathered, Brian straightened his arm, his palm facing the spirit, and scanned her. At first, it was a jumble— fragments of emotion, shards of memories—but slowly, pictures began to form in his mind.

He wasn't standing in Emily's house anymore. He was outside, in the middle of a colonial village, its streets muddy and lined with tiny wooden houses. Torches flickered in the night, and a mob stood in a circle, jeering and shouting. In the center, a young woman—her hands bound behind her back, her swollen belly visible beneath a tattered dress—was dragged toward a wooden stake.

Esmeralda.

Brian's breath hitched as the image of her execution flooded his mind. The accusations rang out—witchcraft, they called it. Her crime, using herbs to help women with childbirth, but superstition and fear had condemned her. She screamed for mercy, for her unborn child, but the mob showed none. They lit the fire. Brian could feel the heat, the smoke stinging his eyes, powerless to stop it.

Suddenly, the scene shifted. Esmeralda's spirit, burning with anguish and fury, refused to leave this world. She clung to the only thing she could—the land where her unborn child was torn from her. Centuries later, she found Rose, a hurt and innocent spirit, trying to connect with her mother Emily. She wrapped herself around her, believing Rose was the child she had been denied.

Brian gasped as the vision broke, the cold of the living room crashing back into him. His legs nearly gave out, but he steadied himself. His head throbbed with the intensity of the psychic connection.

A gust of icy wind ripped through the room as Esmeralda's form began to take physical shape, her hollow eyes locking onto Brian. She appeared just as she must have centuries ago—pale and gaunt, her ragged clothes darkened with the soil of the grave. In her skeletal arms, she cradled a baby.

"She is mine," Esmeralda hissed, her voice sharp and bitter like iron scraping against stone. "I will not lose her again."

Brian stepped forward, forcing himself to stay steady as cold dread crawled up his spine. He knew to be careful, or Esmeralda's rage would escalate.

"Esmeralda," Brian said gently, though his voice trembled under the strain of keeping calm. "I know the pain you've carried. But Rose... is not your child."

Esmeralda's eyes narrowed, her form flickering with anger. The air grew heavier.

"She is mine!" Esmeralda's voice was desperate. "You will not take her from me!"

"Brian's heart pounded in his chest. "But your real child, Esmeralda... she's been waiting for you. She's been crying for you all this time."

The icy winds swirled faster, more violent. Brian pressed on, his words cutting through the howling static that filled his ears.

"Your baby," Brian continued, "thinks you abandoned her. She's waiting for you in the light. Esmeralda... she needs her mother."

A whisper drifted into Brian's mind—be a conduit.

Brian swallowed hard, stepping closer, his voice soft but urgent. "I know. You didn't leave her. I can help you find her, Esmeralda. She's waiting for you... crying out for her mother." He extended his hand, steady despite the overwhelming force of the spirit's presence. "Take my hand, Esmeralda."

Esmeralda hesitated, her hollow eyes flickering with uncertainty. But she moved closer, her skeletal hand reaching for him. When her cold, ethereal fingers touched Brian's, he entered her netherworld.

With his free hand, Brian swept the air in front of him until he felt a tug—a connection between her netherworld and the next. He held still, letting the energy gather, connecting.

Esmeralda's form shimmered, her face contorting between sorrow and confusion. "I hear her, she cries for me?" Esmeralda's voice was fragile, trembling like a mother's.

The vengeful rage that had once fueled her began to dissolve. Her eyes, once hollow and dark, softened for the first time in centuries. The icy grip on the room loosened, and the static in Brian's ears began to fade.

"Yes," Brian said, his throat tightening. "She's waiting. But if you stay on this plane, you'll never hold her. She's in the light. You just have to go to her."

Esmeralda's rage and sorrow that had kept her tethered to this world began to crumble like the walls of an ancient fortress, finally giving way.

Then, with a trembling breath, she whispered, "I see her..." Her gaze lifted toward something beyond the room, beyond this world. A faint glow began to radiate from her, and the cold that had pervaded the room receded, replaced by a gentle warmth. "It's my baby... she's calling me."

Tears welled up in Brian's eyes as he watched Esmeralda's transformation, the ancient spirit finally understanding the truth. The light in the room grew brighter—soft, golden—and Esmeralda's form began to dissolve into it, fading like a breath on the wind.

"Go to her," Brian whispered, watching as Esmeralda vanished completely into the light, her spirit finally finding peace after centuries of suffering.

The room fell silent. The static was gone, the chill replaced by warmth.

Brian slumped to the floor, it was over. Esmeralda had moved on to be with her child.

Emily entered the room, holding Anna close to her chest, her eyes wide and filled with disbelief. "Is it... is it over?" she asked, her voice trembling.

Brian nodded, wiping the tears from his face. "Yes," he said softly, his voice thick with emotion. "She's gone. She's with her baby now."

Emily let out a small breath of relief, looking down at Anna, who had fallen asleep in her arms. Carefully, she placed the baby in the crib, tucking her in gently.

"Rose wants to be remembered, not forgotten," Brian said quietly, watching Emily. "That's why she came here. She wanted you to remember her, but she got caught in Esmeralda's grip."

Emily's eyes filled with tears, "My poor baby Rose," she whispered, her voice cracking. She turned toward the empty room. "I'm so sorry, Rosie. Mommy's so sorry." Her voice wavered as she spoke into the quiet, "I'll never try to forget you again. Mommy still loves you, Rosie. You were my first love. It hurt so much... I tried to forget, but I shouldn't have. I'm so sorry."

"Maybe," Brian said gently, "tell Anna about her older sister when she's old enough to understand."

Emily nodded, brushing her tears away. "I will, I'll tell her all about Rose. And I'll hang up her baby picture next to Anna's so she will always be remembered." She returned to the crib and lifted the sleeping baby into her arms. "And you," she nuzzled the baby, "you shall be Anna-Rose from now on. I will never, ever forget my baby Rose again."

As Brian stood there, his heart full, a sudden burst of light appeared in his mind—a brightness more intense than anything he had ever experienced. Along with it came a voice, a whisper, yet powerful: Protection... protect yourself.

The words echoed through him, their meaning clear. Something beyond this moment was coming. Something that would test him again.

"Brian? Brian, can you hear me? *Brian!*"

I fell into myself. "Yes," I said, catching my breath.

"Am I doing the right thing?"

"Yes, I can feel her spirit is happy."

"I smell flowers. Is that my imagination?"

"It's a sign, a good one. Rose is letting you know she is happy."

* * *

That night, for the first time in a week, I slept deeply. When I woke up at 8:00 a.m., the sun filtered through the blinds. I stretched, feeling unusually rested, and made my way to the bathroom. Afterward, I headed downstairs, expecting the usual quiet morning routine.

But when I walked into the kitchen, I stopped short. My father was sitting at the table, his hands folded in front of him, waiting.

"Hi, Dad," I said, surprised to see him. "When did you get here?"

He smiled, "A little while ago. I let myself in."

"You want coffee? I'll make a fresh pot," I offered, moving toward the counter.

"Sure," he said, his voice calm, almost serene.

I started the coffee maker, the familiar gurgle filling the silence. I couldn't shake the feeling that something was amiss. "What brings you around so early?" I asked, pulling out the pre-measured coffee packet.

He hesitated, then spoke softly. "I came to apologize."

I turned, staring at him. "For what?"

"For not believing in you. For not supporting you growing up. I didn't know any better. I didn't listen to your mother."

I leaned against the counter, watching him closely. This wasn't like him, showing up unannounced and talking like this. "So, the Carter case changed your mind about psychics and the paranormal?" I asked, trying to understand the shift.

He gave a slight nod. "That's just the tip of the iceberg, really." His fingers drummed softly on the table, the familiar nervous habit I knew so well. His sadness seemed etched into the lines of his face, and for a moment, I felt an unexpected pang of empathy for him.

"Dad, it's okay. A lot of people don't believe in psychic phenomena. You're not alone in that."

He shook his head, "No, Brian, it's not okay. You're gifted, and I... I held you back. Your mother told me you had the shine ever since you were a baby. When you were five, you could find things—things that were lost. Whenever I misplaced my keys, you found them. God only knows how, but you did. And it scared me."

I turned back to the coffee pot, trying to process his words. "Scared you?"

"When our neighbors lost anything," my father continued, "they came to us so you could find those things for them too."

I frowned, "Hmm, I do remember something about that."

"You still have your gift," he continued, his voice soft. "Look at you—you found that boy in just a few hours. But back then, I didn't think there was any money in being a psychic. I didn't want you to end up like some palm reader in a circus, so I discouraged you from using your gift. When you grew older, old enough to understand, I ridiculed anything to do with it. I thought I was helping you, not hurting you."

I let his words sink in. "That explains a lot."

He shifted in his seat, looking uneasy. "Your mother wanted me to tell you some things—"

"Mom?" I interrupted, my heart catching in my throat. "You waited thirteen years after she passed to tell me? What is it?"

Before he could answer, my cell phone started ringing from my upstairs bedroom. The sound made me wince. "Damn it," I muttered. "I'll be right back."

"Don't answer the phone," my father said, his voice unusually sharp.

"What?"

"Don't answer the phone," he repeated, his eyes locking onto mine. "Let it go. Stay here and talk. We have much to talk about."

I shook my head, "And I want to hear it all. Especially about Mom. Just give me one minute, and I'll be right back."

"No," he pleaded, "If it's important, they'll call back. Please. Stay. This... this is our time."

"Dad, I have to answer that call. I've got a lot happening right now—a big book deal, a possible movie deal, and this ghostwriter situation. It's all on the line. If it's not a matter of life and death, I'll get rid of them, I promise. I'll be right back."

"Now is our time," he said again.

"What are you talking about? We've got all day." I waved him off, walking out of the kitchen. "My schedule's clear. We can spend the whole day together—breakfast, lunch, dinner."

I ran up the stairs to my bedroom, the phone still ringing. Snatching it off the nightstand, I glanced at the caller ID—Mrs. Esposito, my father's neighbor.

"Hi, Mrs. Esposito," I said, slightly breathless. "What can I do for you?"

Her voice trembled on the other end. "Brian, I'm so sorry to call you... it's your father."

"My father?"

"Mi Hijo, the ambulance just left. They were too late. I'm so sorry to be the one to call you, my son..."

Her words barely registered. My eyes glanced at the security alarm panel on the bedroom wall. The system was still armed. No doors had been opened. No one had come in.

My heart stopped. My legs started shaking so violently I could barely stand. The phone slipped from my hand, clattering to the floor as I bolted down the stairs, three steps at a time.

"Hey, Dad!" I shouted, running into the kitchen. But the room was empty. The chair he'd been sitting in was still pulled out from the table.

"Dad!" I screamed, my voice cracking. "Dad, come back!"

Chapter 3 - Reunion

Brian stepped into the chapel of Decker's Funeral Home, where his father's body lay in quiet repose. To his surprise, the room was packed. Startled, he backed out to glance at the sign beside the door. It was his father's name. He hadn't known his father had so many friends.

Terry Cott emerged from the crowd, dressed in an elegant black dress with a single pearl resting on a gold chain. "How are you holding up?"

Brian managed a faint smile. "I didn't expect anyone to come—let alone this many. I haven't planned anything for afterward."

"Mike's Diner is half a mile down the road," she offered gently. "They have a large back room. You could call and see if it's available."

"Thanks," he murmured, fumbling for his phone. "What's the cross street there?"

Without a word, she placed a steadying hand on his. "Would you rather I call?"

He nodded, relieved. "Thank you."

Terry held his arm gently, guiding him toward the front. His father had pre-arranged everything. Brian rested a hand on the polished cherrywood coffin, looking down at his father lying on white satin sheets.

He took a seat beside Terry in the front row. After a moment, the funeral director, Janice Evans, leaned over to whisper to him, "Mr. Miller, your father requested arrangements for refreshments at Andrew's Restaurant on Hylan Boulevard after the burial. I can announce it at the end of the service, unless you have other plans."

Brian nodded, relieved. "No, that's perfect, thank you."

As Janice stepped away, Terry rummaged through her handbag. *Didn't see this coming, huh?*

Brian answered. "No, I didn't."

Terry looked up. "Didn't what?"

He paused, then gestured vaguely to the room. "See this coming."

Her eyes widened as she grasped what had happened. "You're going to have to stop doing that," she whispered, shaken but trying to smile.

Brian shrugged, sheepish. "Sorry... it sounded vocal."

She shook her head, muttering, "Jesus Christ, Brian."

Just then, the parish priest from St. John's Lutheran Church took the podium, his voice rising over the quiet crowd as he began the eulogy.

"Theodore was imperfect in his life; you live life in the flesh, and there is sin in the flesh. But Theodore is beyond sin now and, in death, has become perfect in the eyes of our Lord."

Brian leaned toward Terry and whispered, "Is he drunk?"

"Shush," she replied, pressing a finger to her lips.

"What is he saying—that my dad's only perfect now that he's dead?"

"Just listen," she murmured. "It's about religious redemption."

"More like too much sacramental wine."

A stifled laugh escaped her, but she quickly recomposed herself as the priest continued. After the service, mourners approached Brian, offering their condolences and sharing quiet memories.

At three o'clock, they buried his father at Resurrection Cemetery on Sharrott Avenue. Later, at the restaurant, guests lingered, recounting stories of his father's generosity and humor. As Brian listened, he realized his father had lived a life with its own connections, joys, and kindnesses—much of it unknown to him. He felt a bittersweet pang of regret, wishing they could have shared more, but knowing that now, it was too late.

That evening, as Brian pulled into his driveway, he and Terry stepped out in silence, the weight of the day hanging heavily between them.

"I think you should take a few days off before the final read-through on the book," Terry suggested, closing her door.

"It's as good as it's going to get. I'm not reading it again," Brian replied, activating the car's alarm with a faint beep. "The book doesn't feel important anymore."

Terry turned, frowning. "What are you talking about? Don't go wobbly on me now. This is big, Brian—a life-changing opportunity."

He sighed, shaking his head. "I let that goddamn book ruin an opportunity I'll never get back."

"What opportunity? What are you talking about?"

"I don't want to talk about it," he muttered, brushing past her.

"Just like that?" She stepped in front of him, blocking his path to the door. "Don't blow this, Brian. Look, I can talk to the editor.

Considering everything... maybe I can push the deadline back a week. Give you time to grieve.”

She was being kind in her own direct way, but he could feel something else shifting in him, something bigger than the book.

“My path’s changing,” he murmured.

Terry’s eyes searched his face, but before she could respond, a young woman appeared, walking up the driveway toward them.

“Excuse me,” she said softly. “Are you Brian Miller?”

He glanced at her, surprised. “Yes.”

Her voice trembled. “I need your help. I think... I think I’m possessed.”

Brian exchanged a glance with Terry. “My path.” He nodded to the woman. “Let’s go inside.”

* * *

Terry paced across Brian’s kitchen, her voice low but steady as she spoke into her phone. “Tom, he’s legit. The real thing.” She lowered her voice to an urgent whisper, “His father just passed; it rattled him.”

“A psychic who couldn’t foresee his own father’s death?” Tom replied, a sarcastic edge in his voice. “Not exactly a ringing endorsement.”

“You’re not listening,” Terry insisted. “He read my mind. Not guessed—read it. There’s no other way to explain it.”

A pause crackled on the line. “What exactly did he ‘read’?”

“He heard my thoughts and answered me, as if I’d spoken them aloud.”

“Maybe you were subvocalizing. Like those people who mouth words while reading. You might not even realize you’re doing it.”

Terry shook her head, her tone adamant. "I wasn't subvocalizing, and my head was turned away."

Tom exhaled sharply. "Look, if Brian can't keep his commitment, we'll lose traction. We're already advertising his book for the fall. If he delays, we'll bleed money on marketing we can't recover. I can't sell a postponement to the board; if he's out, I have to pull it."

"Give me a week, Tom. I'll work with him, make sure it's ready."

She ended the call, took a deep breath, and walked back into Brian's study.

"It sounds more like a haunting than a possession," Brian was saying, seated behind his desk and scribbling notes.

Terry slid into the chair next to the young woman and dug out her mini recorder. "Do you mind if I record this? Just for my notes—if things escalate, it'll help me keep track."

The girl nodded, wide-eyed. "Sure. I just want this... whatever it is... to stop."

"Kasie," Brian said gently, "are you okay with Terry recording our conversation?"

Kasie nodded, glancing briefly at Terry.

"I'm Terry," she introduced herself with a small smile. "Why did you come to see Mr. Miller?"

"She's been having dreams of a man pursuing her," Brian explained. "At first, she thought it might be possession, but from what she described, it sounds more like a haunting."

Kasie shrugged, looking down. "Why would he wait till now?"

Terry leaned forward. "Has anyone else noticed anything unusual?"

"No, just me," Kasie replied, her voice tight. "But my parents... they've been weird about it. They even had me see a shrink for a while. Didn't help."

"What did the psychologist say?" Brian asked.

Kasie rolled her eyes. "Some bullshit about unresolved issues."

Brian considered this, then asked, "Did you buy anything around the time this started? Something that belonged to someone else—a vintage item, maybe, like a doll or jewelry?"

Kasie shook her head. "No, nothing like that."

Brian nodded thoughtfully. "May I hold your hand?"

Kasie stood, stretching her hand out across the desk. Her skin was warm and soft, as he'd expected. He closed his eyes, centering himself.

After a moment, he released her hand, opening his eyes. "I'm not sensing anything ominous... but there's definitely a vibration coming from you."

Kasie looked at him, puzzled. "A vibration? What does that mean?"

"It means there's something there, though I'm not sure what. Maybe if I saw your home—your room—I could get a sense of whether something's attached itself there."

"Kasie, could you state your name and age for the record?" Terry asked, pointing her mini-recorder toward her.

"My name is Kasie Armstrong. I turned eighteen last month."

"Eighteen, that's good," Terry said, then continued. "Just to confirm—I have your story right that you're having dreams where a man is trying to catch you?"

Kasie nodded, tension flickering across her face.

"So... why is that paranormal?" Terry asked.

Kasie threw her hands up. "See! That's exactly what my parents say."

Brian shot Terry a pointed look, his eyes sharp. Terry held her hand to her chest, mouthing, "Sorry."

Standing, Brian moved around his desk and took Kasie's hands in his. "Kasie, I believe your experience *is* paranormal." He glanced at Terry, then added, "There's a difference between dreams and visitations. Dreams fade when you wake up, but visitations stay with you—clear as day. You remember every detail, the scar above his eye, even down to the pores on the man's skin."

Kasie looked relieved but uncertain. "I only have three hundred dollars saved, and my parents... they won't pay anything."

Brian nodded, giving her hands a reassuring squeeze. "I'm not charging you. Consider it a student discount. Let's see where this leads and get to the bottom of it."

"When can you come to my house?" Kasie asked.

"Now is as good a time as any. Did you drive here?" Brian replied.

"My friend dropped me off. She lives a few blocks away on Victory Boulevard. Her mom's seen you a few times. That's how I found you; you're impossible to locate otherwise."

Brian gave a slight smile. "The people who need to find me, find me." He glanced at Terry. "You want to come along?"

Terry hesitated, then nodded. "Er, yes. Of course."

During the drive, Brian learned a bit about Kasie's family: she was an only child, and her parents, Edith and James, were wary of anything remotely paranormal. He pulled up in front of a blue, two-story house with aluminum siding on Arden Avenue in Eatonville.

"Let me talk to my parents first, then I'll come back for you," Kasie said, stepping out of the car and hurrying into the house.

As they waited, Brian turned to Terry. "Let's get a little closer. I want to see if I can pick up on anything."

"Good idea," she replied, following him as they strolled along the sidewalk in front of the house.

"Anything?" she asked.

"It's vibrating," he murmured, brows furrowed.

"What does that mean?"

He shrugged. "Means there's something here, but I can't read it clearly yet."

Moments later, Kasie reappeared on the front porch, followed by her parents. Her father was tall and reedy, with a bald spot and what remained of his hair jet black. He wore a casual green short-sleeved shirt, a gold watch, and white sneakers. Her mother was shorter and full-figured, dressed in a brown blouse with a deep V-neck, tight black slacks, and multiple shiny rings on each hand.

Kasie looked apologetic as she walked over to Brian and Terry. "I'm sorry. My parents... want you to leave."

Mrs. Armstrong stepped forward, her expression hard. "You should be ashamed of yourself, taking advantage of a teenager—filling her head with this paranormal nonsense."

Mr. Armstrong's gaze narrowed. "If you ever come to my house again or speak to my daughter, I'll call the police. She lives under my roof, and I'll decide what's what. You understand me?"

Brian placed his foot on the bottom step, but a sudden wave of intense apprehension made him sway. Grabbing the wrought iron railing, he steadied himself, pulling forward. "Wait—there's a misunderstanding here."

"There's no misunderstanding," Mr. Armstrong snapped, stepping closer. But Brian sensed something beneath the anger—a current of fear, a hesitation.

Mrs. Armstrong placed a hand on her husband's chest, holding him back. "Get off our property and stay away from my daughter, or I'll call the cops."

Terry took Brian's arm, gently pulling him back. But Brian didn't move immediately; he held up his hands in a seemingly defensive gesture, subtly scanning the couple. Terry noticed the slight, deliberate movement of his hands and understood—he was reading them. *You sly bastard,* she thought.

Brian rejoined Terry on the sidewalk. As Kasie's parents retreated into the house, Kasie approached them, her face apologetic. "I'm sorry. I didn't know they'd react like that."

Brian tilted his head thoughtfully. "Does the man in your dream call out to you, as if in pain?"

Kasie's eyes widened. "He does. Who is he?"

"I'm not sure," Brian replied. "But I can try to find out if you still want to continue."

Kasie nodded. "I do."

"Good. Let's keep this quiet—no reason to upset your parents more." He handed her his business card. "Call me Monday, and I'll let you know if I find anything."

Kasie took the card, her expression grateful. "Thank you."

"Phone and text only, okay?" Brian said, turning to walk back with Terry. Together, they headed for his car.

Did you sense anything?" Terry asked as they walked back to the car.

"I sensed Mr. Armstrong is terrified," Brian replied. "As in, ready to shit- his-pants afraid."

"And Mrs. Armstrong?"

"No, not at all. I didn't pick up any fear from her. What did you notice?"

"Me?" Terry raised an eyebrow. "You're the psychic."

"So, you didn't notice Kasie doesn't look like either of them?"

Terry blinked. "Ah, no, I didn't. I was a little busy watching Mr. Armstrong, who looked like he was about to swing at you."

"Details, Terry. Even the non-psychic ones matter."

"Anything psychic?" she pressed.

"A man's face. And upstate New York."

She looked at him, skeptical. "And what are we supposed to do with that?"

"Get a detailed map of New York State."

When they reached the car, Brian dangled the keys toward her.

She crossed her arms. "I'm your writer, not your driver."

"Got it," he replied, unlocking the doors with a click.

They drove in silence for a few minutes, the tension easing as they left the Armstrongs' neighborhood behind.

"We need to finish your book," Terry said finally.

"You've got everything. It's all in your court."

She shot him a glance. "You still need to proof the galleys for the book."

"I've read it five times already. But if you insist, I'll put everything else on hold and give it my undivided attention."

"We're still in this together, right?"

Brian pulled into his driveway, nodding. "No issue. And thank you, Terry. Today would've been a lot harder without you."

He closed the car door and started toward the house. "I'll read it tonight. If I don't call you, it's good to go. Good night."

"What about the girl?" Terry called after him.

He turned back, his expression unreadable. "I'll handle it from here."

Terry imagined a line of best-selling novels stacked like dominoes on a table. His cases could spawn a whole series of true-crime paranormal books, movie tie-ins, maybe even a TV show. "This story with Kasie could be another book, if we keep working together."

Brian shook his head, a rueful smile tugging at his lips. "Just finish the one you've got."

"I want to know what happens with Kasie," she pressed.

"I'll text you," he replied, keying in the code to unlock his front door.

Terry hurried up the path after him. "Will you wait one goddamn second? Talk to me! Maybe I can help."

Brian turned, an eyebrow raised. "You've made it clear you don't want to assist me."

"No, damn you," Terry snapped, stomping her foot. "An *equal partnership.*"

"Equal?" he replied, sarcasm dripping. "Are you psychic?"

"No, but I'm analytical. I have connections and years of investigative journalism under my belt."

"And yet, you missed that Kasie doesn't look like her parents."

"Because I was focused on Mr. Armstrong, I thought he was about to deck you!" she shot back. "Besides, imagine how much stronger your stories could be with me writing a firsthand account."

Brian rubbed his chin thoughtfully. "I can see the value in that," he said slowly, "but I need an assistant, not an equal. An equal means constant debates about which path to take."

"That hasn't been an issue."

"It would be," he replied, tapping his temple. "Look, you're almost done with the book; after that, you're free to choose your path forward."

"What is it with you and these 'paths'?"

Brian laughed. "My new worldview."

Terry crossed her arms. "Fine, I'll be your personal assistant and writer. But I want fifty percent of all royalties moving forward."

"Forty-nine," he countered, "to avoid the whole 'endless debate' thing."

Terry grunted in frustration. "Did you know I'd agree?"

He shrugged, a glimmer of a smile. "I had a feeling."

"If we're going to be partners, I want the truth," Terry said, her tone serious.

"You'll get it," Brian replied.

She hesitated, then pressed on. "My original research said you were a fraud."

He nodded. "Your research was right. I was."

"But... you're not now?"

"No. I don't think I ever really was, to be honest."

Terry frowned. "That's confusing."

Brian sighed. "Growing up, my father constantly discouraged me from using my gift. He ridiculed me so much I buried it."

"But it's back now—how?"

"The Carter case. James Carter had put a gun to my head, demanding I locate his son or he'd blow my fucking brains out. That life and death pressure... it brought my gift back to the surface." Saying it aloud, Brian felt a wave of relief. For the first time, someone else knew the full story and that made him feel lighter.

Terry's eyes widened. "Holy shit. You never mentioned that! Wow. Can we put that in the book?"

"No," he said, shaking his head. "We agreed to keep the gun out of the story."

"That's a shame—that's pure gold. So, you've been faking it all these years?"

"Mostly. When I look back on my shows, there were times I felt I actually tapped into something real, moments I couldn't explain. But I rationalized them away. Then my dad... well, he came to me before he died, apologized for what he'd done. Said my mom always knew I had the 'shine.' After that, I realized I was faking being a fake. If that makes any sense."

Terry looked at him with a touch of awe. "Lucky, he said that before he passed."

Brian gave a dry huff. "That's... a story for another time."

She watched him closely. "You sure you're okay with work? You just buried your father."

"Work is all I want to do right now," he replied quietly. "Stay busy, stay distracted—I don't want to think about him just yet."

...

Inside Brian's house, Terry set out to prove she could pull her weight in this partnership. She printed a multi-page, high-detail map of New York State, taping the sheets together until it spanned his kitchen table.

Brian laid the map flat and took a round crystal pendulum from his pocket, a fine silver chain trailing from its end. He held the chain lightly between his thumb and index finger, positioning the pendulum a few inches above the map.

Terry watched, brow raised. "I thought you'd just run your hand over the map looking for a 'hot spot.' How does the pendulum work?"

Brian sighed, placing the pendulum down, his expression taut.

"Just details for the book," Terry stammered. "This isn't how you found Johnny Carter, right?"

"No. This approach fits the job at hand."

"Could you explain?"

Brian nodded reluctantly. "It's a way to focus. The pendulum itself isn't magical—it's a focal point. My mind directs my hand, and my hand guides the pendulum subconsciously. It's like a backdoor into psychic abilities."

"Five minutes ago, you told me you'd been faking it all these years. So, how'd you become an expert in psychic phenomena?"

"Because I studied it my whole life. Couldn't leave it alone, no matter how my father tried to shut it down." He gave her a level look. "If that satisfies your curiosity, may I get on with it?"

"Yes, of course. Sorry."

Learn by observation, for Christ's sake, he thought.

Terry gave him a sidelong glance. "I'll try."

"Try what?"

"To learn by observation," she said.

Brian stalled. He laid the pendulum down and excused himself, stepping into his den to collect his thoughts. *She heard my thoughts. Now what?* He concentrated. *Terry, come here. I need you.*

No response.

Okay, she didn't hear that. What's the difference? He replayed the earlier moment in his mind, wondering if the irritation he'd felt had somehow carried the thought to her.

Returning to the kitchen, Brian picked up the pendulum again. He held it above the map, watching as the circles it drew grew smaller and smaller until it hovered directly over Saranac Lake.

Fifteen minutes later, Terry returned with a four-page map of Saranac Lake, taped together and spread across the kitchen table. Brian held his palm just above the surface, slowly moving it until his hand felt heavy over an area near School Street.

"This seems to be it," he said, pressing his finger onto School Street.

Terry frowned. "But we don't know what we're looking for."

"Sure we do," Brian replied with a faint smile. "Something on School Street."

Terry pursed her lips and nodded.

"You dig; I'll rest," Brian said.

"Rest from what?"

He sighed. "I'm drained. It pulls the life out of me to tap into..."

"Into what?" she prompted, her tone softening.

He shook his head. "I'm not sure. Maybe my father's death is catching up with me. I'm still figuring it out."

Her expression shifted with a hint of sympathy. "I forgot. You rest—I'll do the research."

Brian nodded gratefully and headed upstairs. In his bedroom, he barely managed to reach the bed before he collapsed, exhaustion overtaking him the moment he closed his eyes.

...

Terry discovered that Saranac Lake didn't have a dedicated local newspaper, so she turned to the archives of the *Adirondack Daily Newspaper*, which covered Saranac Lake. The paper's archives spanned over a century, and while they were all online, the search function didn't allow for specific location searches. She'd have to go through the records day by day. Starting from the beginning meant a daunting 36,500 searches. *Yeah, no.* Kasie's haunting started a few months ago, so she decided to work backward, beginning six months ago and scanning each paper daily.

After a while, Terry headed upstairs and found Brian fully dressed, shoes on, and fast asleep on top of his bed. Not wanting to intrude, she knocked softly on the open door.

Brian stirred, blinking his eyes open. "How long was I out?"

"Fifteen, twenty minutes. I found something," she said clearly.

Brian rubbed his eyes, sitting up. "You can come in. I won't bite."

Terry stepped inside, glancing around at the dark oak dresser and the intricately carved headboard. She traced her fingers along the grooves, admiring the handmade look of the chisel marks in the wood.

"You found something that fast?" Brian asked, swinging his legs over the side of the bed and standing.

Terry shrugged. "Found an obituary. Adam Chester, fifty-three, lived on School Street—died of a heart attack. Thought you'd want a look before I kept digging."

They headed downstairs, where Brian started a fresh pot of coffee. Terry took the newspaper copy to his office, enlarging the image before returning to the kitchen.

She handed him the pixelated printout. Brian squinted. "Could be him."

She nodded as he laid the picture flat on the table and held his hand above it.

"Anything?" she asked.

"Yeah, I think so. You've got his name—let's find his address and hit the road."

"Seriously? Saranac Lake's over six hours away. Ever heard of a telephone?"

"I can't charm anyone over the phone."

"Who exactly are you planning to charm?" she asked, arching an eyebrow.

"Won't know till I get there." He grinned, unbothered.

Terry sighed. "Look, I know this case is exciting, but we're so close to finishing the book. If this ends up being a wild goose chase, we'll have wasted days."

Brian met her eyes, smiling. "Endless debates."

"Shit!" She rolled her eyes.

He leaned forward. "This is the real deal, Terry. Make your choice—are you in or out?"

Her mind raced. *If this were a dead end, he'd sense it. He's the real deal—I keep saying that, so why am I still doubting?* Her pulse quickened at the thought of diving into this lead, of chasing down another story. *Worst case? I lost a few months. But if I'm right...* She could already feel the thrill of the journey ahead. With a grin, she slammed her coffee cup down, a bit of coffee sloshing onto the map.

"In."

Terry booked two rooms at The Hotel Saranac.

The next morning, they started their trip to Saranac Lake. They agreed to listen to an easy rock station on Sirius radio. A compromise between Billie Eilish, enjoyed by Terry, and 80s Pink Floyd rock by Brian.

Terry felt comfortable driving Brian's Lincoln, the ride was smooth and solid. They stopped for lunch at a highway dinner. The food was surprisingly good.

Terry pulled in front of the house on School Street. Brian stepped out of the car and walked to the front door of a ranch-style home. A woman answered the door. Brian made a quick assessment: black blouse and slacks, widow, gold crucifix around her neck, religious, age mid-fifties, hair dyed chestnut brown, five foot one inches, 135 lbs, income level, mid-middle class.

"Can I help you?"

Brian smiled. "Mrs. Chester, my name is Brian Miller, and this is my assistant, Terry Cott. We're from New York City. I wonder if I can speak with you for a few minutes."

"In regard to what?"

"I'm working for my client in New York City. In my investigation, you came up as a possible lead. Can we talk?"

"This isn't going to take long, is it?"

"No, a few minutes is all, may we come in?"

A voice from inside the house yelled, "Mom, who is it?"

"Visitors," she called back. Mrs. Chester opened the door, "Okay, come in." The entrance led into a green-carpeted living room. The upholstered couch with a beige paisley pattern sat in front of a fully mirrored wall.

Terry and Brian sat on the couch. Mrs. Chester sat across from the sofa. Brian picked up a framed photograph from the end table. He showed it to Terry. His finger on the man next to Mrs. Chester in the picture. He nodded.

"How can I help you?" Mrs. Chester asked.

"My client may have a connection with your husband."

"Who is your client?"

Brian quickly assessed his options; lying wasn't one of them. "My client is an eighteen-year-old girl from Staten Island.

"What are you saying?" Mrs. Chester rose from her chair. "Has this girl accused my husband of something?"

"No, nothing like that."

"Then what exactly?"

"Honestly, I don't know. That's why we're here. Looking for the connection."

Mrs. Chester's eyes drew into slits, and her lips pulled tight.

"If you don't know, what led you here?"

"I'm a psychic—"

"Oh my God, leave." Mrs. Chester pointed at the door. "You think you're going to sell some old fool widow messages from the beyond. I won't listen to any of your crap."

"No, wait, let me hold your hand to read you, and I'll prove it."

"If you touch me, I'll have you arrested for assault."

"Okay, no touching," Brian said, holding up his hands. "Let me stay for a few minutes and see what I can sense."

"Get out!" She pointed at the door again. "I'm not buying anything you're selling. My husband's dead, and he's not coming back to me."

"He didn't come back to you; he came back to my client."

"He's the real deal," Terry interrupted, placing her hand over her heart. "I would never say that if it weren't true."

Mrs. Chester looked to the floor, thinking a moment, then up toward Terry, "You researched my family, haven't you?" she said softly. "You know about my kidnapped daughter. What is this? Some sort of elaborate plot to extort money?"

A young man, about fifteen years old, rushed into the living room. "Mom, what's wrong?"

"Nothing, they are leaving."

The boy's eyes widened. "I'll get Dad's gun!"

Mrs. Chester spun to face her son. "Don't you dare touch Dad's gun!" Then turned back to Brian and Terry. "Now! Out!"

The boy ran upstairs.

In his mind, Brian saw the boy rushing into a bedroom, pulling open a drawer. "We're leaving," Brian yelled, moving toward the front door.

Terry turned around at the doorway. "You mentioned a kidnapped daughter; we don't know anything about your daughter."

"Stop the act. You both are disgusting human beings, coming here at a time like this with your fairy tale stories."

"We don't want any money. We're working a case."

"Sure, tell that to your next patsy." Mrs. Chester slammed the front door in Terry's face.

Joining Brian by the car, "You certainly charmed the shit out of her," she said, beeping the car alarm off and unlocking the doors.

"Can't charm everyone."

"Did you pick up any vibes inside the house?"

"No, I was too distracted by her screaming spit in my face."

Terry chuckled, "No non-psychic clues either, I gather. What was our goal here again?"

"Gathering information. I didn't anticipate such a strong emotional reaction."

"Shit, we should have mentioned the Johnny Carter case, maybe she heard of it. Or at least to Google it to see we're legit."

"Yeah, good idea, next time," Brian answered. "I didn't plan this well."

"We're learning." Terry shrugged. "Where to, boss?" Terry started the car.

"Hotel, let's check in and see what we can find out about her daughter."

The red brick exterior of the Hotel Saranac on Main Street had an old-world charm to it. The steps to the lobby were white marble. White double doors opened automatically as they approached the entrance.

"This is better than I expected," Brian said, taking in the hotel's lobby.

"I scheduled a spa appointment for myself tomorrow morning."

Brian shook his head.

* * *

After settling in her room, Terry dialed her friend in the NYC police department.

"Hi Kevin, how's my favorite copper?"

"I'm okay, sweetheart, and you."

"I need a favor, can you run a search on an Adam Chester. He lives in upstate New York. His wife's name is Janice."

"Terry, you know special favors are reserved for women I'm sleeping with."

"You cheated on me Kevin, we're over, we're not going back."

"I was a fool, I admit that. But I can't keep doing you favors whenever you call."

"Yes, you can, Kevin, you want to know why? Tommy saved your life in Afghanistan, yeah? But you couldn't save his life, when he needed you, could you? Then you fucked Tommy's little sister and broke her heart. So, by my accounting, you'll always do me the favor, whenever I ask, if not for me, then for Tommy, am I right?"

"Yes...you're right. I will," Kevin answered. "Always."

■■

Terry met Brian in the lobby, and they entered the hotel's restaurant. The bar and grill had a pleasant wood plank floor and various-sized tables placed in the dining area—a row of high tops close to the bar, medium-sized tables for four scattered in the mid area, and a long table that sat twelve people in the center.

They sat at a table for two by a window with a view of an expansive lake. Brian ordered a rib-eye steak medium rare, and Terry ordered shrimp scampi.

"I guess we should try accessing the newspaper again and looking back to see anything involving the Chester family and their daughter," Brian said.

Terry picked up a slice of Italian bread and buttered it. "Eighteen years ago, their baby daughter, Melissa, had been kidnapped. Case never solved."

"What? How do you know this?"

"I have a connection with the NYPD. I called him when we hit the hotel, and he searched. He called me back a few minutes later and said it popped up on his screen."

"Kasie is Melissa?"

"Could be? Would explain why the Armstrongs didn't want a psychic sniffing around their house."

Brian nodded. "Can your friend do a DNA match-up?"

Terry smirked. "Yeah, I asked him that too. He can't. Need to deal with the Saranac police department."

"Great."

"I caught something in the Chester house, did you see it?"

Brian shrugged.

"Don't you think Kasie looks a bit like Mrs. Chester?" Terry said with a self-satisfying smile.

* * *

Brian decided to travel downstate by train to get a DNA sample from Kasie while Terry stayed at the hotel and enjoyed its amenities. Brian preferred the train to flying. An anachronism to the past. He found traveling by train pleasant, no security checks, slower, but he enjoyed the ride. He found a seat by a window and settled in.

Kasie met Brian at Grand Central Station in Manhattan. She held a zip-lock bag containing her hair samples.

Brian looked inside the polybag. "I need the root of your hair for a DNA analysis."

"Hair root?"

"Yes, you must pull out your hair by the root, keeping the root attached."

"Why? What's this about?"

"It's about DNA matching. Do you know if you are adopted?"

Kasie's eyes opened wide in surprise. Brian decided to backpedal, rather than ask questions. "Best not to go into it until I know more. You need to hurry. I must get back on the train for the return trip."

Kasie grabbed some hair close to her scalp and pulled them out. "Ouch...This hurts, you know," she said, pulling out a few more strains of her hair.

"I know. I think that's enough."

###

Brian and Terry walked into the Adirondack Central Police Station the next day.

"This is going to be fun," Terry whispered, walking through the front doors.

Brian exhaled, "Not too much, I hope."

They ended up in the office of Detective Garrett. He was a rookie cop at the time of the incident, but he was on the original case. Detective Garrett frowned at Brian, his arms folded across his chest as he swiveled in his chair. He tapped some keys on his keyboard, looked at his computer monitor, and then at Brian.

"Okay, your story checks out. You're a psychic from the city. You think these hair samples from an 18-year-old girl in Staten Island are the Chester baby from 2002?"

“That’s correct.”

“What’s your angle here?”

“No angle, I’m here to help.”

“Yeah, I see; finding that Carter kid got you notoriety and a book contract. Can’t be that you’re looking to make another score, right? Maybe think we’re a bunch of country bumpkins up here.”

“I already proved I’m legit. My investigation led here. I’m following the trail of clues.”

“Psychic clues, am I right?”

“Right.”

“Only clues a swami like you can obtain.”

Brian shut his eyes and nodded. He looked at the detective and said, “I’m sorry to have wasted your time, detective.”

“Door’s to your right, swami.”

Terry stood abruptly. “We have the DNA. What more do you want?”

“You have hair samples for DNA? Don’t you know we check DNA by using cheek swabs or test tubes full of spit? That’s how it’s done. Not with some dodgy hair samples from God knows who and where.”

Terry snatched the polybag containing Kasie’s hair off the detective’s desk. “You could say no, without insulting us. Is this how you treat all people who come for help?”

“Just the ones who are running a con, missy.”

“How dare you accuse us of that. You know nothing about us.”

The detective stood, placed his hands on his desk, and leaned forward. “I suggest you leave before I arrest you.”

Terry held her ground. "For what, telling you the truth?"

"I'll put you and your boyfriend in lock-up right now if you don't leave." The detective placed his hands on his hips.

Brian pulled on Terry's shoulder and whispered, "Time to go."

Terry turned and led Brian out of the detective's office. In the hallway, Terry ignored the eyes, following them out of the station.

They walked along the chain-link fence leading into the parking lot.

"What's our next move?" Terry asked.

"Back to Mrs. Chester."

"Why?"

"You've seen how angry she gets. She went from zero to homicidal in two seconds. She was literally spitting in my face as she screamed at me."

"Yeah, so."

"Well, if we can direct her anger to the police, we might be able to get them to do the DNA test."

"I see," Terry agreed, nodding.

"Our goal is to sufficiently motivate Mrs. Chester to push the police department in that direction." The grin across Brian's face was bordering on a malicious smile.

"Oh, dear God." Terry's hands covered her face, and she shook her head.

"Let's light this fuse."

...

Brian rang the doorbell for the second time.

Mrs. Chester opened the front door. "Jesus Christ, what is wrong with you people? Leave before I call the police."

"We just came from the police. We have this DNA sample." Brian held up the polybag with Kasie's hair. "They refused to test it to see if it matches your baby's DNA."

"We tried not to bother you again, Mrs. Chester," Terry added.

"We gave them the hair sample for DNA analysis. There's this Detective Garrett at the station; he threw it back at us." Brian said.

"Detective Garrett." Mrs. Chester repeated.

"Yes, it was Detective Garrett," Terry said confirming. "He said he would throw us in jail if we bothered him again with Melissa's DNA sample."

Mrs. Chester slowly reached over and took the polybag offered by Brian. "My daughter?"

Brian nodded. "Might be."

"We need to test for a DNA match to be sure," Terry added. "The police are blocking us."

Mrs. Chester clutched the polybag to her chest and let out an involuntarily sob. She regained her composure quickly. "Carl!" Mrs. Chester shouted into the house. "Get my bag on the kitchen table." Then, she turned to Brian, tears welling in her eyes. "I'll get it tested."

Brian and Terry jumped into their car and tried to follow Mrs. Chester to the police station. They made it to the station in time to see Mrs. Chester stomping up the stone stairs to the entrance.

When Terry and Brian entered the police station office, Mrs. Chester stood toe-to-toe in the police station lobby with Detective Garrett. The wide-eyed desk sergeant remained silent and didn't move from behind his desk. Brian was impressed with the volume of sound emanating from the 5-foot-1-inch frame of Mrs. Chester. Her face was red, veins in her neck distended, and spittle flying from her mouth into Detective Garrett's face.

"What has your entire police department done for the last 18 years? NOTHING! Not One God Damn Thing!"

Detective Garrett held up his hands. "You're upset. You need to calm down, ma'am."

Mrs. Chester placed her index finger an inch away from the tip of Garrett's nose. "Don't you ma'am me, you son-of-a-bitch. You get one fucking clue in 18 fucking years, and you don't follow it. Get Detective Ellis."

"He retired five years ago, ma'am. And you need to calm down before I need to—"

"Need to what?" She screamed louder. "Arrest me? Go right ahead. You think I'm making noise now? Wait until I have my lawyer and cry to the news. Go ahead, you incompetent bastard." She held her wrists out in front of her. "Arrest me. I'll expose you for the bumbling keystone cop that you are. Get Ellis."

"He's retired. I'll handle the DNA analysis."

Mrs. Chester moved her head inches away from Garrett's face. "You! You think I'm going to trust you?"

"Ellis is retired. I can't call him in."

"Bullshit. I see him all the time in ShopRite. Get him on the fucking phone; I'll talk to him myself. Now, and I mean pronto."

Mrs. Chester, Terry, and Brian waited in an interrogation room for Detective Ellis, who arrived 30-odd minutes later.

Detective Ellis stood about 6 feet, with white hair on a lined face that had seen one too many things in his life. His hands were knotted and work-worn, skin rough and calloused as he shook Brian's hand.

Honest was the word that came into Brian's mind as their hands met.

"Janet," he said, wrapping his arms around Mrs. Chester. "I'm sorry about Bo. He was a good man."

She returned his hug. "We need to take care of this, Louis."

"We will." He turned to Terry. "And who might you be, young lady?"

"I'm Terry Cott. I'm a writer working with Brian."

"Newspaper?"

"No, books, biographies mostly. I'm detailing Brian's cases."

"Right, Garrett brought me up to speed. Janet, did you have to dress him down in front of the precinct?"

"The way he spoke down to me, calling me ma'am and shit, treated me like I'm some doddering old fool."

Ellis nodded. "We'll do the DNA."

"Louis, I don't want Garrett anywhere near this case."

"I concur," Brian added. "If he's involved, the test will come back negative."

"Hey! What are you saying?"

"He's saying he doesn't trust the man," Mrs. Chester interrupted, "and neither do I. You know that."

"I remember. I think I can get this through without waiting months to reopen your case."

"You will do this, personally, for Bo?"

"Yeah, some friends up in the county lab owe me a favor or two. I think I can make this happen, unofficially."

"And do it personally?"

Detective Ellis smiled and nodded. "I'll deliver the package myself. Results will take a few weeks, depending on when they can squeeze in the tests."

"I'll come with you, so you don't have to make that drive alone," Mrs. Chester said.

...

Two weeks later, Brian and Terry were sitting at the dining room table. Brian handed Terry the pre-press book from the publisher across the table.

"Looks fine to me. Go with it," Brian said.

"Are you happy with the results?"

Brian considered the question, "I am," he answered with a nod. Brian's cell phone rang. "It's Janice Chester." He said as he accepted the call. "Hello."

"Mr. Miller," Janice's breathy voice came through the phone. "It's her. It's my baby…" She began to sob.

The sound of static and the phone rustling a bit, a few whispered words, then, "Mr. Miller, this is Louis Ellis. I was the detective assigned to this case."

"I remember you, detective."

"Mrs. Chester is a little too out of sorts to talk, but she wants to come downstate immediately to meet her daughter."

"Don't you need to contact the local police?"

"Yeah, if we want to delay things for a few weeks. I'm thinking we come down, they meet, and we can wing it from there."

"My client knows nothing about this."

"You haven't told her?"

"Didn't see the need until I knew for sure. Maybe give me a few days to speak to my client and bring her up to speed."

"We can do this soft, or we can do it hard. We're coming downstate. If you do not bring us to Mrs. Chester's daughter, I'll have you arrested for aiding and abetting kidnappers."

Brian hung up his phone.

"What happened?" Terry asked.

"It's Mrs. Chester's daughter. They want to meet Kasie as soon as they can get here."

"Can you blame them?"

Brian's phone rang. He looked at the number and rejected the call.

"I haven't said anything to Kasie. I have to tell her that the man in her dreams is her biological father, who recently passed. I asked for some time to prepare her, but Ellis said no. I have to spring all this on Kasie. The kidnapping, her parents are not really her parents, who, as of now, have some real legal issues to contend with. And oh yeah, by the way, here's your real mother.."

Brian's phone rang again. He looked at the number and rejected the call again.

"Who's calling you?"

"I don't know, Chester or Ellis."

"Why aren't you picking it up?"

"Ellis threatened me if I didn't bring them to Kasie, so I hung up the phone."

"Is that wise?"

"Probably not," Brian chuckled, "but right now, he's busier dealing with a hysterical Mrs. Chester than with having me arrested."

"What are you going to do?"

"Let him suffer. See if his attitude softens up the next time we speak."

"You got a mean streak."

"Yeah, I'm funny like that when I'm threatened. In the meantime, let's contact Kasie."

Brian's phone rang again. He rejected the call without looking. He glanced at his watch. "If they leave Saranac now, they'll arrive around 5 tonight."

Brian texted Kasie. She agreed to come by his home after school.

At 4:15 pm, Kasie sat at Brian's dinner table with Brian and Terry, hands folded. Her eager face stared at Brian in anticipation.

"This is a bit difficult." Brian began.

"What did you find?" Kasie moved her folded hands from the table and placed them in her lap.

"The man chasing you in your dreams, I believe, is your biological father, who passed a few months ago, around the time you started having your dreams."

"What about my parents?"

"I don't know. I'm assuming you're adopted."

"If I'm adopted, then my biological parents gave me up."

"No, that's not how it happened. Eighteen years ago, during a home invasion in upstate New York, a baby girl was kidnapped."

Kasie stood, holding her hand to her chest. Her eyes widened. "I'm the baby?"

Brian winced. "It appears so. Please sit."

"I can't...." Kasie began gulping in the air as she circled the dining room table.

Terry held the trembling Kasie in her arms. Terry looked over to Brian and said. "We're with you. You're not alone."

Brian nodded.

Kasie pulled back to look into Terry's eyes. "What do I do?"

"Sit." Terry guided Kasie back to her chair.

Kasie sat and looked at Brian, "Are you sure?"

"As sure as your DNA."

Kasie stood again. "Oh my god. My parents never said anything."

Terry asked, "They never said you were adopted?"

"Please sit," Brian said.

Kasie said, "I'm going home."

"Your biological mother," Brian glanced at his watch, "will be here any minute."

"What? Isn't that my decision to make? Who to let know or not? Isn't this my right? You're working for me, aren't you?"

"I am. But to check your DNA, we had to put a few balls in motion, and once in motion, we can't stop them."

"But I don't know what I want to do?"

Terry moved in front of Kasie. "It's going to be okay."

The doorbell rang. Brian took a deep breath and stood.

"I don't know who this woman is. I don't want to meet her. I just want to go home."

"Let's take it slow. I'm right here," Terry said.

Detective Ellis and Mrs. Chester entered the living room. Her eyes found Kasie. She hesitantly moved toward her. Tears rolled down her cheeks. She raised her hands and touched her face. "Melissa."

"My name is Kasie." Kasie shook her head. "I don't know you."

Mrs. Chester sobbed, tears flowing down her cheeks. She nodded. "I know... I know. But not a single day has passed that I haven't thought about you. And now," she smiled through the tears, "here you are."

Detective Ellis approached Brian. "If I had any authority, I'd haul your ass to jail."

"Well, you don't. I have some 18-year-old single malt scotch in my den if you'd like a drink instead," he said. Then nodding toward Kasie and Mrs. Chester. "We should let them have a moment."

Ellis nodded. Brian led him into his study.

It was nearly 5 PM, and the warm light cast dancing shadows on the den's dark-oak wood-paneled walls. A few bookshelves stood tall against the panels, filled with hardbound volumes and various curios, all meticulously arranged, hinting at Brian's refined yet eclectic taste.

Two expensive leather armchairs—deep burgundy and well-worn—faced each other across a small mahogany table. A matching lamp with a brass base cast a mellow glow, emphasizing the room's intimate, almost mysterious ambiance.

Without a word, Brian poured the scotch into crystal tumblers. The caramel-hued liquid caught the lamp's light, reflecting its purity. He handed one to Ellis. They raised their glasses in an unspoken toast and each took a long, slow sip.

They swallowed their first round quickly, and Brian poured a second. Ellis settled back into the leather chair, letting the scotch's mild smokiness roll over his tongue.

"So," Ellis began after a moment's contemplative silence, "what's going to happen?"

Brian leaned forward, resting his elbows on his knees, the corners of his mouth quirking. "Why ask me?"

"You're the psychic." Ellis's tone was half a tease, half serious.

Brian huffed, setting his drink on the table. "Okay." He unfocused his eyes and pulled in a deep breath. "I see Kasie spending the summer with Janice. They will grow close, but not mother-daughter close. That'll take years. Did you dig up anything on Kasie's adoptive parents?"

Ellis took a pull from his drink, his grip tightening around the tumbler. "I found out that the lawyer who handled the adoption is dead, so there are no records as to what arrangements were made."

Brian reached for his glass, swirling the golden liquid slowly before lifting it to his lips. "I feel the father knows more than he's letting on. He's smart enough to keep his mouth shut. The mom is oblivious to whatever deal was made at the time. They'll go to court, get their wrists slapped for an illegal adoption. Kasie was never abused, and there's no tie-in to the kidnapping. They were just a desperate couple looking to adopt a baby and were taken in by a shady lawyer."

Ellis nodded gravely, shifting in the leather chair. "The scumbags who kidnapped Melissa clocked Bo on the head with a tire iron. Cracked his skull open. If Janice didn't get home when she did, he would have died. The attack left that scar above his eye."

"Yes, I've seen that in his picture."

"What you don't see in the picture is the years Bo tormented himself for not protecting Melissa. He blamed himself, was in therapy for years, and tried to commit suicide twice."

"He's at peace now, Detective."

Ellis's expression hardened. "But that scumbag lawyer and everyone else involved got away with it, never suffered for all the pain he caused."

In a fluid motion, Brian swept his arm out in front of himself. Then he recoiled his arm, grimacing like he'd just received an electric shock. He shook his hand vigorously. "Don't worry, Detective, he may be dead, but he didn't get away with anything."

Ellis frowned. "Sure...sure," he said dismissively, taking a sip of scotch.

Brian pinned Ellis with a steady gaze. "I'll tell you something else: he's waiting for Garrett to join him." He winked, but there was nothing playful in his eyes.

Every hair on Detective Louis Ellis's body stood on end. That truth of justice in the hereafter shook his soul. He also confirmed what he and Janice Armstrong suspected, that Detective Garrett was in on it. "What about me? Tell me my future?"

Brian scanned Ellis, in his mind's eye, his future was black. The veins supplying his heart with blood were almost closed. Brian circled his hand an inch away from Ellis's chest over his heart. He felt he could dissolve the fatty blockages.

"I'd like to try something?"

"What?"

"I guess you'd call it a healing. I need to put my hand on your chest."

The detective straightened, setting his scotch aside. "What are you going to heal?"

"Your heart. I sense a blockage. I think I can dissolve it."

Ellis offered a brief, tight smile. "I appreciate that." Detective Ellis said with a smile. "But I'd prefer my regular MD to do my heart healing if you don't mind."

"You don't have the time."

Ellis's eyes widened, a protest forming on his lips. But something in Brian's demeanor—his calm certainty, made Ellis pause. He leaned back in his chair, exhaling shakily. "I don't have time to see my regular doctor, is that what you're saying?"

Brian looked Ellis in the eyes, "That's exactly what I'm saying."

Ellis stared at him, the tension in the room coiling like a spring, "Then I'd say give it a go."

Brian placed his hand on Ellis's chest above his heart. He imagined energy from the palm of his hand, gently dissolving the fatty blockages in the veins.

Ellis didn't feel anything at first. Then he felt a gentle warming in Brian's hand that grew in intensity, his hand becoming hotter than humanly possible. The heat migrated inside his chest, surrounding his heart.

"I feel like there's a blow torch on my heart." Ellis's heart began pounding hard. "Are you sure you're not killing me?"

"Shush." Brian reprimanded. The blockage was in the veins supplying his heart with blood; he focused his energy inside the veins, located on his heart's surface.

Brian remained focused, visualized the veins feeding Ellis's heart, and narrowed in on the location of the blockages he had sensed earlier. He directed the searing heat, invisible energy, into those damaged pathways. After a few minutes, he pulled his hand away and sank back into his chair.

Ellis stared at him, chest heaving, "Did it work?" he asked.

Brian scanned him. He caught a flicker of a future image: Ellis and Janice Armstrong together—content, very much alive. Brian nodded, "Yeah, it did."

"Are you okay? Your face turned to ash."

"I need to rest." Brian said, leaning his head back against the worn leather chair. "I hope there aren't any repercussions."

"Repercussions?" Ellis's hand found the crystal tumbler of single malt on the table beside him.

"Well," Brian murmured, pinching the bridge of his nose in exhaustion, "if it was your time to go, and I changed fate, so to speak, there might be repercussions."

"From who?" Ellis demanded

"Ever hear of chaos theory? You know a butterfly flapping its wings in Brooklyn today will change the weather pattern in China a month from now."

"What the fuck are you talking about?"

Brian shook his head, grinned, and shrugged. "Forget it."

Against the backdrop of the ticking grandfather clock, he murmured, "Well, thank you—whatever that was."

"You're welcome," Brian said softly.

Chapter 4 - Blood Magic

Brian strolled down Lincoln Ave. on his way to the Vintage Bistro to meet Terry. He passed a palm reader's shop, its neon sign shaped like a crystal ball with a psychic middle eye that flickered.

Brian looked inside. He felt drawn to the palm reader's store, but ignored his impulse and continued walking. Pausing outside the diner, he remembered to *trust himself.* He checked his watch; it was 7:15 pm. He shook his head, turned around, and headed back to the store.

The door jingled a copper bell as he opened it. Unlike most mystic shops, this one wasn't small, cramped, and dark. Instead, the room had even lighting from several torchiere floor lamps with marbleized amber glass shades and a few lit candles.

The scent of sweet incense hung in the air. On the shelves were crystal balls in various sizes, incense, tarot cards, amulets, charms, and potions. A woman entered from a back room through a beaded curtain hung in the doorway.

She wore a cream-colored medieval overdress with trumpet sleeves, a translucent chemise boho, with a neck scoop that exposed her ample bosoms.

"Hi," she greeted him warmly, "can I help you?"

She was beautiful, with long flowing red hair, soft skin, and a graceful figure, easy to admire in her form-fitting medieval outfit. "Yes." Brian smiled. "I'm looking for an amulet to protect me from evil spirits."

Brian sensed a rock in a natural setting with a waterfall, interpreting it as a symbol of confidence and an understanding of nature.

"I make custom amulets to fit everyone's needs; have a seat."

She gestured toward the palm reader's quintessential round table in the corner, purple cloth, and crystal ball.

Brian was surprised; he hadn't noticed the table when he entered the shop.

A deck of tarot cards was laid to the left of the glass orb. "Sit," she said. "Let me look at your palms."

They sat. She took his hand and gazed into it, tracing the lines in his palm with the tip of her finger. Then, she said, "Hmmm", tilting her head to the side, looking as if she were trying to figure out a puzzle in his palm.

"Just so you know, I don't believe in palm reading or the supernatural," Brian said.

She met his eyes. "Liar," she whispered, then looked toward his palm again. "The first thing I'll do is draw something from you." She took one of his hands and held it a few inches above the table. Her other hand began circling above his hand.

Brian could feel her finger circling, tickling his palm, even though she wasn't touching him. The feeling penetrated further, and he pulled his hand away. "That's enough."

"Your power's blocked. I may be able to help you unblock it if you allow me to."

Brian took both her hands in his.

"What are you doing?" She asked, then flipped her hair back casually and smiled.

"I'm reading you." He tried, but found nothing, all neutral and grey. I'm blocked, he thought, and said, "It's not working."

She shook her head, lips pursed in disapproval, and stared at him intensely. "You're a sorcerer, not a fortune teller. Ask me what you want to know?"

That hit him. I'm a psychic, not a sorcerer. Maybe a psychic is a sorcerer to her. In any case, she's real. That's why I was drawn here. She can read me. "Can you see my future?"

She nodded. "I see the possibilities...."

"What are the possibilities?"

"I see great danger."

Oh, I get it. She wants to sell mystical protection. I'm a fool. Brian smiled. "I see a mistake in coming here." He stood. "I have a meeting I'm late for." He bowed slightly and turned away.

"If you don't want to have a future, then leave," she said. "But I see things that even frighten me."

"What happened to my possibilities?"

"Your future is bigger than you. It affects this world." She looked like she was struggling with the words. "I see why you're so late now. Some people succumbed to dark forces, they didn't want you to have knowledge and abilities."

Brian spoke, "What abilities?"

"Oh my, you are a sorcerer with great power, the Sovereign Sorcerer."

"Wow, you're one heck of a fortune teller."

"I'm not a fortune teller. I am a seer." She stood and took his hand. "This way," she said, leading him to the back room. "I need to be sure."

The cavernous back room stunned Brian, walls of aged stone looming overhead. An obviously warped dimensionality because the room couldn't fit on the city block, let alone behind the palm reader shop on Lincoln Ave. He turned, taking a quick look into the shop, and watched pedestrians passing in front of the shop window.

"Jesus," he said under his breath.

He continued, his steps echoing on the stone floor etched with intricate runes. He tapped the walls, expecting to hear the hollowness of a plaster wall behind tiles, but he didn't. The wall was solid stone, warm and hard. Iron fire lanterns hung on the walls and filled the room with flickering, soft orange light. The air was heavy; it smelled of incense and old paper with a faint hint of smoke. The seer walked to a gargantuan library to the left, containing bookcases filled with thousands of books that seemed to go on forever.

The room vibrated with knowledge and power. She searched the spines and pulled a volume off a shelf. The cover was thick, aged leather, cracked and delicate. She released the leather straps. After flipping through several pages filled with faded handwriting and symbols, she stopped, her finger marking a page.

"Here is what you need: protection for the practicing of magic. I want you to have the book. Learn the spells and study the laws. This volume contains important blood magic rituals."

The page was written in an ancient language comprised of symbols that reminded him of hieroglyphics.

"This isn't my thing. Making potions and casting spells, the eye of newt, toe of frog. I play a mental game."

A smile crept across her face. "Maybe you wouldn't have to play a mental game if you learned to spell."

"I can't read it," Brian said as he lightly tapped the book.

"If you wanted to read it, then you could read it. It starts with intention and comes with study. This will come to you because you are meant for this."

Her appearance began to change. She was no longer the tall, beautiful woman who walked through the beaded doorway and greeted him. She was shorter, heavier, and older. He stepped back abruptly. "Hey, what is going on here? Who are you?"

"I could maintain my spell. But I think letting it fall, is better for you to understand, yes?"

Brian spoke, "Your spell?"

"If you had not seen, how would you believe it?"

He hesitated; her beauty had taken him in. His guard was down when it ought to be up. "Sorry. I misjudged you."

Her eyes glowed red as her outline faded. Brian felt drained, and he could no longer see her.

* * *

Brian dreamt he was in a woodshed. The door opened, and a large, fat man entered and approached a workbench. He was in the shadows. Brian's perspective was from the ground. The man hummed a children's nursery rhyme. He turned and walked towards him, beginning to unbuckle his pants while still humming. He came close and said, "Close your eyes and hum this tune." His vision shifted outside the shed; twelve children were holding candles in the night, chanting.

> This old man, he played one,
> he played knick-knack with his thumb,
> in a quaint old house, living
> quiet and alone,
> oh, those young things should have known.
>
> This old man, he played two,
> he played knick-knack, there's a clue:
> with the neighbor's girl, she was
> only eight years old;
> swore he'd take her if she told.
>
> This old man, he played three,
> he played knick-knack, made him tea
> with a honey spoon, he could
> hide the sour taste;
> watch him sleeping as he paced.
>
> This old man, he played four,
> he played knick-knack, wanted more
> so the bedsheets bloomed into
> flower-garden stains:
> crimson petals, cruel terrain.

This old man, he played five,
he played knick-knack, hollow-eyed,
in a basement decked with
rompers, shoes, and bows:
remnants of the ones he chose.

This old man, he played six,
he played knick-knack for a fix
but to fix, he broke
their bodies, every hinge
rusted raw and fire-singed.

This old man, he played seven,
he played knick-knack, no confession
though the streets were fraught with missing-person signs:
wary mothers, candle shrines.

This old man, he played eight,
he played knick-knack, lay in wait
in the playground, smiling,
pockets full of hair,
scoping out his latest snare.

This old man, he played nine,
he played knick-knack, seemed benign
but a gnarled old hand knows
how to lead a child
to the place where it's defiled.

This old man, he played ten,
he played knick-knack once again
singing knick-knack paddywhack,
give the dog a bone,
look how my collection's grown.

Back in the shed, Brian saw a glowing metal brand removed
from a propane torch's flame. The brand was an iron cross. He followed
the brand as it traveled through the shed to a child tied and blindfolded
on the floor. The brand was brought down on a child's breast, and the
child screamed.

* * *

Brian jumped awake, his head pounding. He looked around, he lay naked in bed. The stone walls of the room seemed somewhat familiar. The cast yellow light from iron fire lamps embedded in the walls. He struggled to remember how he got there, and the memory of his dream evaporated. He stood up; the stone floor felt warm to his feet. Dizzy, he sat on the bed, his hands running across the soft, furry pelt on top of it.

A woman walked into the room, naked, with raven hair tossed over her shoulders, porcelain skin, green eyes, and breasts full and luscious. His breath caught in his throat. She put on a sheer white camisole.

"I trust you're well rested, Sorcerer." She walked toward a mirror and began checking herself in the mirror.

"How did I get here? Who are you?" he asked. "Am I dreaming?"

"No, you are awake. I am Morgana..."

Brian stood again, slowly, checking his equilibrium. "Who?"

"I am the one to show you your path." She took his hands in hers.

"Right, I remember, you're the palm reader?"

Morgana turned away from the mirror and walked toward the bed. "Yes, I apologize, the power flowing from you is very seductive. I couldn't stop myself from partaking."

Brian could not pull his eyes away from this perfection of beauty in front of him, he said. "Judging from the situation, I feel I may have gotten the better end of the deal."

She laughed.

Brian felt his face flush. "Where are my clothes?"

She pointed to her dresser, a black piece of furniture crafted from dark wood and accented with gleaming silver hardware. The piece was carefully made, smooth to the touch, and reflected light in a mirror-like fashion.

Brian picked up his shirt, which lay folded on top of the dresser in the way he always folded his shirt, but he did not remember folding his shirt or laying it on the dresser. Under his clothes lay the ancient book he'd forgotten about.

He held up the book. "I'll leave this with you."

"It's yours," she said, caressing her body. "You did such a good job of not reading it." She moved toward Brian. "Try again," she said.

Brian opened the book. The first page now contained two lines written in English.

The secret of Heaven and Earth lies in the light.

Enlightenment illuminates the nine doors to the universe.

He looked into her eyes and noticed a small dot of amber in her right eye; the dot flashed red. Brian turned the page and found more symbols.

"You must want to read the book, to read it, there's no other way. It takes work. It will not always be easy."

"Why?"

"You're the one who must fight the blackness rising over this realm."

Brian shook his head.

"You don't believe me?" Morgana said.

"I am not sure what I believe anymore."

"You will before tomorrow's light. You've seen your future in a dream in my bed, yes? Your father says it was as it had to be." Morgana turned away. She caught Brian staring, "I have nothing more to give you right now, leave."

"What?" Brian stepped into his jeans; he vaguely remembered having a dream with children singing.

"You must walk your path; it will be difficult, but I will help."

Brian reconsidered leaving. Why should I leave this beautiful woman? He pulled off his jeans and lay down on her bed. "Maybe I'll stay."

"Mortals." She said, exasperated. "Get up. Terry is waiting for you, and you're late."

"Late? Can't be. It's not tomorrow?"

"No, it is not."

He glanced at his watch. It read 7:20 pm. Only five minutes had passed since he entered the shop. Five Minutes! His heart began pounding. Something is seriously wrong.

Morgana said, "Take your book, and I will see you again when you need me."

"You need to tell me what's going on?"

"Now is not the time." Morgana said calmly, "Here is a gift for Terry." She handed Brian a gift box.

Morgana grabbed his hand and led him out of her bedroom chambers, into the hallway, down a stone staircase, into the main room, passed the library, and finally to the beaded curtain to her shop. It was still daylight, and through the shop window, people walked past. She placed her hand on the doorknob and opened the door. "Study the book, hurry; Terry is getting ready to leave."

When Brian's foot stepped out of the shop, onto the pavement, he felt a Whoosh, like he had just stepped off a fast-moving walkway. He momentarily lost his balance.

He continued walking toward the Vintage diner, leaving one reality for another.

* * *

Brian was reeling in disbelief as he entered the Vintage dinner. Terry waved from a table near the center of the dining room area.

"What's your hurry?" Terry said. "You're only half an hour late. What is that smell?"

"Maybe this." He held up the ancient leather-bound spell book. Some dark ash fell from the pages onto the white linen tablecloth.

"Definitely that," Terry said, holding her nose. "Did you have to bring it in here?"

"Let's put it in your bag."

"Hell no, I don't want my bag smelling like some ancient Gouda cheese. God only knows what bugs are crawling around in there." Terry stopped a passing server to ask for a plastic bag they used for take-out to hold the book.

"I brought this for you." Brian handed her the white gift box.

"That's so sweet. What is it?"

"Open it and find out."

Terry opened the box and held the necklace. A delicate blue sapphire suspended in an open, curvaceous frame with a chain. "Beautiful," she said, turning it over in her hand, "there's an inscription on the inside."

"Read it," Brian asked.

"I can't. It's tiny symbols." Her voice was a soft echo. "So beautiful... It's enchanting; I can't believe you bought this for me."

"Bought may not be the appropriate term. Let me see the inscription." Brian couldn't read the symbols, but he felt that the characters were a spell for protection.

After dinner, they returned to Brian's home. They sat at the kitchen table, outlining their next book. They decided on the title "Reunion," and it would detail the home invasion and kidnapping of Kasie Armstrong. As they brainstormed locations and names to protect the identities of the people involved, the doorbell rang.

Brian opened his front door.

An attractive woman about thirty-five, with dirty blond hair, wearing tight faded jeans and a form-fitting light blue blouse, asked, "Are you Brian Miller?"

Brian sensed her grief. "Yes, how can I help?"

"My son Tommy has been taken, and you found that Jimmy Carter boy; can you help me find my son?"

"You mean Johnny Carter. Please come in," Brian said, leading her into the interior foyer of his home with polished hardwood floors and mahogany wood panel walls. "What's your name?"

"Cheryl Bigelow."

Brian smelled something in the air that didn't seem right. It wasn't the alcohol, cigarettes, and pot that wafted off the woman; there was something else, something old, malevolent. "Well, Cheryl, have you spoken to the police?"

"No police; I can't. My ex, Vinny, my boy's father, is involved; it's complicated."

"The police need to be brought in on a criminal abduction."

"It's not a crime, at least not yet. Find him, get me to where he is, and I'll do the rest."

Something was off. It wasn't vibrating true. It wasn't her, but like a cloud of malevolence around her. "I can't help until you contact the police."

"Listen," she said, stripping off her blouse, "I'm not in my twenties, but men are still hot for me." She dropped her blouse to the floor and removed her bra. The word "Spellbound" whispered into Brian's head. She placed a hand under each breast, holding them up for him to examine.

Brian's eyes locked on her wrists, a dozen healed cut marks on each wrist and fresh needle marks on her arm. He scanned her body, looking for a mystical marking that may symbolize a binding.

"I don't have money," Cheryl said, "but I will do anything you want, anything, any hole, any time." She unbuckled her jeans and pushed them down, revealing her dark pubic hair. "I will fuck and suck you as no woman has ever fucked and sucked you before in your life; just help me find my son."

Brian said, "Turn around so I can see all of you."

Cheryl did as she was told.

There were no binding markings he could see on her skin.

Terry entered the foyer, catching sight of a naked woman. "What in the world is going on here?"

"This young lady is in desperate need of me to help her find her son."

"I can see that," Terry said.

Cheryl pulled up her jeans and, grabbing her blouse from the floor, threw it on, she said, "I'm sorry, I didn't know you were married."

"I'm not married, and Terry's not my girlfriend." Brian felt a seething wave of jealousy from Terry. Brian said, "Come inside, and we'll see if we can figure something out."

"I really hope you're not this desperate to get laid," Terry said.

Brian turned toward Terry. "You know I can hear your thoughts."

"That wasn't a thought. I said that out loud." Turning to Cheryl, Terry said, "Please go inside; we need a minute."

When Cheryl entered the living room, Terry turned to Brian. "Why are you just standing there letting this woman do a striptease for you?"

Brian moved his mouth close to Terry's ear and whispered. "She's spellbound. I didn't ask her to remove her clothes, but when she did, I looked to see if there were any mystical binding marks anywhere on her body."

"Oh, really?" Terry said, pursing her lips with a frown.

"Really," Brian answered, gently nudging Terry into the living room.

###

They convened around the dining room table. Terry had her notebook on her lap and the digital recorder turned on.

"Tell me what I need to know," Brian said to Cheryl.

"My ex, Vinny, took our son to pay off a debt."

"You are using your son to pay a debt?" Terry asked.

"I'm not; my ex is. He's in trouble with the wrong people and everything's out of control."

"Do you have any idea where your son might be?"

"I know he's been drugged and being delivered to some perv on the island. When I heard them talking about this, I thought they meant some other kid, not my Tommy. The guy coordinating it is this creep named Frank," she said. "He's a nasty bit of work."

"He's on Staten Island?"

Cheryl nodded.

Brian knew he had to take the case. He wanted to make Terry feel she was part of the decision-making process. He turned to Terry. "What do you think?"

"About what?"

"Taking the case?"

"How old is your son?" Terry asked.

"Five," Cheryl said.

"Jesus Christ, of course, take the case."

"Do you have anything of his?"

Cheryl opened her handbag. "Yeah, I keep some of his favorite toy cars; it helps keep him quiet when we go out."

Outside, Brian directed Cheryl to his car, and Terry sat in the driver's seat.

"I have to get a stick from my car," Cheryl said, then ran to her vehicle and pulled out a two-foot-long white stick from the back seat.

Cheryl jumped in the back seat of Brian's car and held the stick in her lap.

Brian turned in his seat facing Cheryl, "What do you plan on doing with that stick?"

"It's how I reason with my ex when words fail me."

Brian grunted, holding Tommy's toy car in his left hand. He relaxed, clearing his mind, and he fell into the car. He heard children chanting, with the cadence of an old nursery rhyme.

This old man, he played one,
he played knick-knack with his thumb,
in a quaint old house, living
quiet and alone,
oh, those young things should have known.

The dream about the children in the shed came rushing back. He pulled himself back from the toy car. A sickness grew in the pit of his stomach. He hadn't experienced that before. He rubbed his belly, healing himself with his hand, and the nausea passed.

The dream is connected. Something's not right. His fear and apprehension rocketed like a moonshot.

"What are you waiting for?" Terry asked.

"I need a moment."

"I'm sorry, take what you need." Terry apologized.

I'm too far in, I have to play it through. Brian swept his right arm in front of himself. He felt a strong pull to the right.

"Go to the corner and make a right," Brian said to Terry.

"Is this how you found Johnny Carter?" Terry asked.

"Exactly."

Twenty minutes later, they pulled in front of an old house, big but splintered, its front porch littered with dried leaves and crushed beer cans. The paint was weathered with flaking edges and curling corners.

The wooded porch steps creaked as Brian, Terry, and Cheryl climbed them to the house.

Brian and Terry stood at the front door. Cheryl hid behind them.

Brian knocked, and a skinny middle-aged man answered the door. His skin was pale, covered in purple bruises, and his cheekbones jutted out as if carved from stone. His eyes were red and sunken, with black bags beneath.

Terry said they were searching for a missing child and asked if he knew anything.

"No, there's no kids around here," The man's voice was dull and sunken like his eyes.

Cheryl pushed past them and screamed, "Where the fuck is my baby, Frank."

The man tried to slam the door closed, but Brian pushed it in. The room was filled with filth and trash, and the smell of decay filled the air.

Cheryl hit Frank from behind with her white stick as he tried to run away. Frank collapsed to the floor midstride. Cheryl jumped on him, grabbed his hair and pulled his head back, screaming into his ear, "Where's Tommy?"

Brian and Terry tried to pull Cheryl off the fallen man.

"Stop," Brian yelled, "you'll break his neck and kill him. You don't want to be brought up on murder charges for the likes of him?"

Cheryl let Brian remove her hand from Frank's hair and let his head fall forward.

"He's in a shed in the backyard," Brian said.

Frank rubbed the back of his neck, nodded, and said, "Yeah, that's right. There in the back."

They released Frank, who scrambled out the front door and continued running down the street.

They exited the front of the house as the sodium streetlights flickered to life, casting an eerie yellow glow. They walked around the house and looked down the driveway leading to the backyard.

Brian's apprehension took another moonshot, and he stopped moving.

Cheryl's hands forcibly hit Brian's back, pushing him forward. "Why are you stopping? My son's in danger. We need to hurry!"

Brian snapped around. "Stop!" Brian's anger emanated with a force so intense that Cheryle fell back into Terry.

Terry walked around Cheryl to Brian. "What are you feeling?" Terry asked.

"Danger." He said and began inching down the driveway.

They turned the corner of the house. There was a large woodshed. Light shone from its tiny window.

"What is that smell?" Terry asked.

"Something rotten, or dead," Cheryl added.

"I don't smell anything," Brian said.

"You're kidding me. My eyes are watering it's so bad."

Brian, Terry, and Cheryl approached the shed. Brian took a few more steps closer.

From inside, he heard a man yell, "Action!" Then, a young child cried, "Daddy, please, stop!"

Brian pushed the shed door open.

Inside, a large, fat man told the child it was time to take his medicine. The boy's father gave the boy a spoonful of liquid. The boy swallowed his medicine. The father pulled down his pants and told his child to close his eyes and sleep. The fat man began humming the nursery rhyme "This Old Man" to himself.

The fat man turned around, seeing Brian, he pointed toward him. The father jumped up from his chair, turned, and started running towards Brian. In an instant, everything stopped and froze in position.

Confused, Brian turned around; Cheryl and Terry were behind him, their mouths agape, immobilized in position. He snapped his fingers in front of Terry's eyes.

She didn't blink.

A voice seemed to come from all directions at once, rumbling and booming like the earthquake of a far-off storm. Its deep foreboding timbre conveyed both an air of wisdom and menace. A strange, unidentifiable accent gave the voice a haunting cadence.

"So, we finally meet, Sorcerer?"

Brian felt a presence behind him and spun around. A hooded figure appeared, clad in black robes, its face hidden in the shadow of its hood, its eyes glowing red, out of the pitch blackness under its hood that should be its face. The figure radiated dark, malevolent energy.

Brian's heart seized in his chest, and his blood turned to ice.

"Sorcerer?" the figure asked again.

Brian's mind froze. His legs wouldn't move.

"I have been waiting a hundred years," the voice said, its long pale finger with a sharpened yellow fingernail extending beyond its robe pointed toward Brian, "for you."

The rumble of its voice was like an echo from eons past, mysterious and otherworldly. It vibrated with power that kept Brian paralyzed in place.

The figure glided closer to Brian.

"You are the Sovereign Sorcerer."

Brian couldn't make out any details; he seemed shrouded in mist.

"You are as weak as a child. No, you are a child. Just a morsel of energy. I am disappointed."

"Energy?" Brian asked, his voice a raspy whisper.

“I will devour you, child, and your friends too.”

The figure snapped forward, and Brian instinctively threw up his hands. But it passed Brian and stopped in front of Terry.

"I shall start with your woman. You can watch as I devour her essence, her soul. She will scream in ecstasy as I rip her body apart, and she will beg me to continue.” The creature’s mist surrounded Terry, then pulled back in. “What's this, a protection amulet?"

Instantly, the figure snapped in front of Brian. "That stench, Morgana, you reek."

The creature sniffed the space around Brian. “You’ve been a naughty, naughty boy, haven’t you, Brian? You lay with Morgana?”

Brian took a deep, cleansing breath and regained the ability to move his legs. The words "be confident" and "negotiate" entered his mind.

“Morgana must have seen us meeting tonight, protected your girlfriend, and made you unpalatable.”

The figure turned to Cheryl. "You, on the other hand, are—"

"Let's negotiate," Brian said.

The figure laughed. "Child, you have nothing to negotiate with."

"I have the Sovereign Sorcerer’s power."

The figure laughed harder. "And what will you do with that, boy? A power you don’t wield or control."

"I'm learning," Brian said.

"If Morgana hadn't marinated you with her disgusting oils and essence, I would devour you. But I can still kill you and be done with it."

"I suppose you could. But what's the fun in that? Besides, if you kill me now, you'll never get to devour my power. You waited a hundred years; what's a few more? Give me the time to learn my craft, fatten myself up." Brian said. "I'll make it worth your wait."

"I'll give you three years."

"Five, I need five years."

"No."

"Are you afraid I'll grow too strong for you to defeat in five years, is that it?"

"Me afraid of a mortal? I'll tell you this, child, you can have your years. It affords time for my minions to play with you. By the time I come for you, you'll be grateful for the release."

"Fine. The mother and child are to leave with me."

"What do you offer in return?"

"Keep the men in the shed; they're yours."

"They're already mine."

"Not if the police come, you will lose them, and others your service. It's a zero-sum game. Permit me to leave with the mother and child; the police will not be called."

"Very well, child, take your little win; it will be the only one."

As the figure vanished into the mist, everyone resumed moving.

Cheryl pushed past Brian, wielding her thin white stick with which she struck her ex-husband Vinny. He fell to the floor, grabbing his forearm and howling in pain. Brian grabbed the stick from her hand as she raised it to hit him again. The thin stick was not made of wood as he thought, but was a heavy iron rebar painted white.

The fat man stumbled backward, pulling his pants up and knocking over the tripod holding a camera. The camera fell to the ground, and the live stream from the camera revealed the ground perspective on a monitor.

Brian stomped the camera, smashing it into the floor, black plastic pieces scattered, and the video feed went black.

"Grab Tommy and get out of here." Brian yelled.

The drugged child was tied in a bent-over position to a black leather bench. Cheryl untied the unconscious boy's hands and ankles and pulled his pants up. Then she hoisted his limp body into her arms and carried him out of the shed.

"Cheryl, I'm sorry, baby." Vinny said from the floor, holding his arm. "I had no choice; it would have been okay, I'd protect him, I swear, baby."

Terry's cell phone was in her hand. "I'm calling the police," Terry said.

Brian took her phone and closed it. He shook his head and said, "No. Don't."

Terry grabbed her phone from Brian. "Are you fucking crazy? These people are pedophiles. We have to call it in. God knows how many kids they hurt."

A luminescent figure of a five-year-old girl appeared before Brian. Her dress was soiled with blood, where no child's dress should be soiled. "Hurry, Brian, he sent a minion, it is coming."

With his eyes fixed on the apparition, Brian said, "I know, but we can't do that. We have to leave now."

The fat man sat in the corner with a sick smile plastered on his face. He started humming the children's nursery rhyme, "This Old Man."

Terry frowned, knotting her eyebrows. "No, I'm calling it in. This is part of a ring. Who knows how big."

Another child apparition appeared outside the door of the shed. The young boy pleaded, "Hurry, it's almost here, hurry…"

Brian placed his hand on her phone. "Look at me," he said. "I'm afraid, and not for our lives but our souls. And if I'm afraid," he said, placing his hand on his chest, "you should be terrified."

Terry looked into his ashen-colored face and nodded.

"Run!" Brian said, grabbing Terry's arm and bolting out of the shed.

"The Sovereign Sorcerer has spoken," the fat man said in a sing-song fashion. "The Sovereign Sorcerer"—he laughed—"has spoken."

Terry and Brian ran out of the backyard and down the driveway. Cheryl and Tommy were in the back seat when they reached the car.

Back home, Cheryl put Tommy to sleep in Brian's guest room, then joined Brian and Terry downstairs in the living room.

Cheryl sat on the couch, trembling and twitching. Sweat beaded on the pale skin of her forehead. She wrapped her arm around her stomach.

"I have to go out for a few hours, but I'll be back for Tommy. I'm feeling sick; I need some medicine," Cheryl said.

Brian nodded. "Let me see if I can help with that." Brian sat on the coffee table in front of Cheryl and placed his right hand on her chest between her breasts. Then he placed his left hand on her back in line with his right hand. He pressed his hands together, generating a warmth between them.

Cheryl said, "Wait. What are you doing…I can feel that going through me."

Brian removed his hands after a few minutes.

Cheryl said, "Oh my God, I feel so much better. I'm not sick. What did you do?"

"I removed your addiction. It will hold as long as you don't use. If you use again, it will return as if it never left."

"Will this stick forever?"

Brian nodded. "For as long as you don't use."

"How can I thank you?"

"Go stay with Tommy, and we'll talk in the morning."

When Cheryl left, Terry asked Brian, "Are you okay?" Terry's face was creased with worry.

Brian felt his life ebbing away, he felt like he was dying. His limbs were weak and heavy. "I'm afraid if I fall asleep, I may never wake up."

"Shit, what can I do to help?"

"Morgana, I need to get back to her."

"Who?" Terry asked.

<hr>

Terry drove back to Lincoln Ave, half a block down from the Vintage diner. Where the psychic shop had been located was now a closed dry cleaner's store.

"Are you sure it was here?" Terry asked.

"Positive."

"Now what?"

Brian huffed, outstretched his arm, and scanned.

"Go around the block."

Terry drove up South Street, and Brian saw the shop. "There it is," he said.

"Where? I don't see it."

"Pull over to the side and let me out."

Terry parked on the side of the road.

"Stay here," Brian said, opening the car door.

Terry watched Brian slowly walk down a dark alley between buildings.

Brian entered the psychic shop. Morgana was waiting.

"Back so soon, Sorcerer."

"I need help." Brian wheezed the words out and coughed. He dragged himself to the round table in the corner and collapsed in the chair.

Morgana sat across from him.

"Did this shop move, or is it my imagination?" Brian asked.

She tilted her head as she studied him. "The shop is where it needs to be when it needs to be. You met whom you are destined to meet, yes."

Brian retold Morgana the night's events, up to healing Cheryl.

"Five years?" Morgana said, shaking her head. "You play a dangerous game with the Specter; you need twenty-five years to learn your craft, fifty to be any good."

"I wasn't in a strong negotiating position. What did you call it, the Specter?"

"I call it Specter, just to call it something. If I knew its name, I would have more power in my incantations to defend myself. There's power in knowing its name."

“I consider myself lucky not getting us all killed, or worse.”

Morgana's eyes glinted with a knowing twinkle, and her lips curled up. “If it wanted you dead, you’d be dead. Yes?” She nodded her head slowly, seemingly in deep contemplation. She exuded an air of calm assurance and certainty and had a secret understanding. “Instead, it wants you to win you in mortal combat so that it can take control of your physical sphere, this realm, and control you like a puppet.”

“Why?”

“You are the Sovereign Sorcerer. You are a Protector. What better way to display his omnipotence than to puppet the Sovereign Sorcerer and do his bidding?”

Brian sat back and thought for a moment. “Why me? Why am I this Sovereign Sorcerer?”

“Your parents’ DNA, at your conception, interlocked and formed a Kolief. The real question is why it took so long for you to radiate and make your presence known to me. You are old to begin your journey.”

“Too old?”

Morgana tilted her head and gave a slight shrug. “I am used to training earlier, after puberty, when the strength begins. Maybe your age can be made an advantage.”

“The more I train, the more powerful I become. Is that it?”

“Approximate, yes.”

“And Spector needs me to engage of my own free will?” Brian asked.

“Yes,” Morgana answered.

“Then I won’t accept; I won’t fight.”

“It’s too late for that.” Morgana shook her head, “You offered the challenge and negotiated the terms, so it is written, so it will be so. The battle will take place five years from today.”

"Do I have any chance of winning?" Brian asked.

Morgana stared; her eyes focused far away. Brian felt there was something, a deep, hidden secret. Morgana was hiding from Spector. That's why her entrance moves. And he's a pawn in a battle between two...what? What are they? Semi-gods, demi-gods, angel, and demon? Eternals? Brian asked, "What do you see?"

Morgana stood and placed her hands on her hips. "I see a chance. But you are depleted, and we need to take care of you now," she said. "Wait," she instructed and walked into her back room. She returned a few minutes later. "Drink this." She handed him a cup with a foul-smelling concoction.

He held the cup of a green-brown liquid. It smelled rotten and rancid. "I can't drink this."

Morgana huffed a breath, "Drink or die, both are your paths to travel."

It tasted like rancid oil, thick, warm, and heavy; it coated his throat like a blanket. Then, as the liquid hit his stomach, he felt his energy rise from his groin and spread throughout his body. "Wow, I feel better."

"It's only temporary," Morgana said. "You need to feed." She placed the palm of her hand on Brian's forehead. "When you return to the car, place the palm of your hand on Terry's forehead and say this incantation."

"I won't do that."

"Then you will die."

"Motherfucker. Is there another way?"

"You can't go around healing people and not expect to replenish your energy."

Brian nodded, "That's my price to pay, not anyone else."

"You healed that drug-addicted female and gave that child his mother back. You saved her child from being raped and marked for life.

If that isn't worth a year's penance of life, I don't know what is. Take what you need from Terry to work. Then replenish fully from the child you saved."

"I can't harm a child," Brian said.

"You think this is a negotiation, it is not. You are taking what you had given to save him."

"It just doesn't sit well."

"There's more," Morgana said, placing four amulets on the table. "You need protection. Don't think the dark forces will wait until you are ready to battle. Now that I can sense you, they can sense you too. You need the pure blood of an innocent to complete the amulets; this is one ritual in blood magic."

Brian returned to the car. The effects of Morgana's tea were quickly wearing off.

As Brian sat in the passenger seat, Terry shook her head. "You still look like death," she said.

Brian nodded. A thin sheen of sweat covered his pale face. His lips were tinged blue. "Close to it. May I touch you?"

Terry frowned. "Do you think this is an appropriate time for that?"

Despite his nausea and pain, Brian chuckled and shook his head. "I need to take a little of your life force."

Terry's eyebrows knotted, she leaned in close, and took Brian's hands into her own. "How much?"

Brian flinched. Her touch burned his skin, and he released a short groan. "Enough to get home and replenish the energy I had given Cheryl from Tommy."

"The child, no, you can't."

"Then I'll die."

Terry hesitated for a moment, then sighed. "Take it from me. Take what you need from me."

"Are you crazy? It would take a year off your life."

"I'm young and strong. Rather me than Tommy, please. That boy has been through enough."

Brian wasn't strong enough to argue; he placed the palm of his right hand on Terry's forehead, his left hand on the back of her head, aligned with his right. He focused his mind and repeated the incantation, "Bozam rahjen endor." He felt the power flowing from her to his hand and into his body.

Terry's eyelids flickered; her breathing slowed, and she relaxed in the car seat and began moaning sensuously.

Her energy was liquid, flowing to him like river water downstream. The power was seductive, and he became afraid he may not be able to stop, so he willed the flow to taper off and close the conduit. He had done it. He removed his hands from Terry. Her eyes were closed; she seemed at peace and calm. A single tear slid down her cheek.

"Terry," he whispered.

Terry released a long sigh. Her eyes opened, and her hands grasped her head. "My head is pounding."

"Side effect."

Rubbing her temples, she said, "I felt my energy leaving, but I didn't care. I became so sexually aroused; I never wanted you to stop."

"It's seductive on both sides," Brian said.

"I never felt so loved before. Do you feel the same towards me?"

Brian looked into her eyes, "It's the shine. You're bewitched. It's temporary, it will pass in a few days, a week at most."

"I don't care what it is, I will do anything you want?"

###

Back at the house, Brian opened his safe in his study and removed his emergency funds of twenty thousand dollars in cash. He brought the cash into the kitchen, where Terry was making coffee.

He aligned the four amulets on the table.

"Each amulet needs the blood of an innocent."

Terry removed the automatic lancet they purchased from the twenty-four-hour Delco Pharmacy on Highland Blvd.

"It's time to wake up Cheryl." Brian said.

"You sure this can't wait until morning?"

"No, seconds count. If we're attacked, we have no protection."

* * *

Brian opened the door to the guest bedroom, using the hall light to see inside the room.

He knelt by the bed and touched Cheryl's shoulder.

Opening her eyes, Cheryl asked, "Is everything all right?"

"Come downstairs, we need to chat."

Brian explained that powerful supernatural forces were gathering against them, and he needed her and Tommy's help.

"I have this lancet to draw blood from Tommy's fingers," Terry explained. "He wouldn't even feel it really. The chambers in the amulets are small. I think we can fill them with one prick of each finger."

"It sounds crazy, but no less crazy than anything else that happened tonight, and I owe you, so okay," Cheryl said.

"Let's get this done," Brian said.

Cheryl's long blonde hair swayed as she climbed the stairs to the second floor and returned with a sleeping Tommy in her arms. She sat at the kitchen table.

Tommy's face was calm, his eyes closed, and his lips turned slightly into a smile. His hands were small and delicate, like they might break if squeezed too hard.

Terry cleaned the tip of Tommy's index finger with an alcohol pad. She placed the lancet against the skin and then triggered it.

Brian hated doing this; he told himself it was only a small amount of blood. The child's body would replenish it in a few days. He held the amulet under Tommy's finger as Terry milked the blood from Tommy's fingertip and filled the amulet's small chamber.

They performed the same operation for the three remaining amulets. When finished, Terry watched Brian open the ancient book, and align the amulets before he recited an incantation while cupping his hands over the charms.

Cheryl carried the still-sleeping Tommy back up to bed.

Brian placed one amulet in each far corner of his house. Finished, he walked into the living room and collapsed on the couch.

Cheryl walked downstairs and entered the living room. Terry rested in a recliner as Cheryl joined Brian on the couch.

Brian felt a wave of jealousy from Terry. Was it a core feeling from her or the bewitchment he couldn't determine?

Brian picked up the four stacks of crisp one-hundred-dollar bills he had left on the coffee table.

"This is twenty thousand dollars; I want you to take it and start a new life, away from New York," he said to Cheryl.

"My life is here."

"If you stay, you'll fall back in with the old people, old routines, start using again, and destroy your life and Tommy's."

"You don't know that," Cheryl said.

"But I do; I'm a psychic."

"He is," Terry agreed. Brian felt Terry would say or do anything to push Cheryl out and away from them.

"I don't have anywhere to go," Cheryl said.

"Texas," Brian said with a firm nod. "Austin, Texas. You can take my car. I'm buying a new one. I'll sign over the title to you."

"Why are you doing this for us? You don't even know me."

"You're on my path. God put you and Tommy in front of me for a reason. Besides, it's the right thing to do."

Brian caught Terry out of the corner of his eye, jerk back when she heard him say God, and then sat up straighter.

"Vinny is Tommy's father. He'll follow me or file a lawsuit if I take Tommy away."

"You're worried the man who pimped your five-year-old son out to be raped on a live stream to all the pedophiles on the planet is going to lawyer up for child custody?" Terry asked.

"Not when you put it like that," Cheryl agreed.

"Tell no one you're leaving, vanish. In the morning, get in my car, put the address for this motel in Austin in the GPS, and leave."

"I'll need to get our clothes at the apartment."

"If you go back to your apartment, you'll get trapped."

"I have some clothes I can give you." Terry interjected.

Brian continued, "Stop in a small town along the way and buy clothes. Stop for the night in a motel, and keep traveling until you reach Texas."

"You're serious."

"Like a heart attack. I want you and Tommy to wear these amulets around your neck." Brian held out two leather necklaces, each with a black stone encased in a gold wire setting.

"Where did you get those?" Terry asked.

"Another gift from Morgana, she sees things."

"Are these protection charms?" Cheryl asked.

"No, cloaking charms," Brian said. "They'll make your location invisible to seers. Wear them now and never take them off."

"Really?" Cheryl frowned.

"Wear these as if your lives depend upon it," Brian said, looking into her eyes. "Because they might."

She nodded slowly, taking one necklace from his hand and putting it around her neck. She felt a tangible sense of safety and protection as the black stone charm settled against her skin.

Terry and Brian waved as Cheryl drove out of his driveway and down the street.

"Is she going to make it?" Terry asked.

"I think she is."

She paused, then asked, "And Tommy?"

"He's with his mother. They left the monsters behind; he'll be fine."

"And Vinny?"

"Odds are he won't."

"Good," Terry said.

Chapter 5 - Morgana's Baby

Chapter 5 - Morgana's Baby

Brian stood behind Morgana as she looked through the books in her medieval library. She pulled a book off a thick stone shelf.

"This one is for you," she said, turning around to hand Brian an ancient leather-bound volume.

The flickering orange light from the flame torches danced upon Morgana's porcelain skin. Brian glanced at her ample cleavage behind the book she offered. Morgana's clothing was more revealing tonight than was usual for her. Not that he minded the show, but it made him suspicious.

Brian accepted her book with reverence. "Isn't it dangerous to use torch flames for light in your library? All your books could catch fire."

"These are cold flames, light with no heat," Morgana answered, placing her hand into the flame of a torch, "See."

Brian placed his finger gingerly into the flame; there was no heat; instead, the flame tickled his finger with static electricity. "Is there anything in here that isn't magical?"

He opened the book and carefully leafed through the ancient parchment pages, yellowed with age. He came upon the first spell in the book. Reading the symbols was becoming easier. As his eyes stayed fixed upon a symbol, it would morph into legible English text, and he began to read.

By whispered word and silent vow, let this bond be forged.
I name you, [Name], and dissolve the boundary that guards your slumber.
Within the quiet halls of your dreams, I enter unseen,
Moving through the corridors of your mind.
I guide your thoughts to my will.
So be it said—so be it done.

Brian touched the hieroglyphics on the page as he closed the ancient book and looked up. Shadows flicker across the walls, cast by the cold torch flames.

"The Dreamwalker's Spell," Morgana said, stepping closer. You are not experienced enough for the words alone to open the door to dreams. You must use the ritual and repeat the incantations to focus your power like an unattuned weave-bound neophyte."

Brian lowered his gaze; the intonation in her voice was far from subtle.

Humbling himself, he confessed. "I can't read these lower glyphs. Is that the ritual?" Brian asked.

Morgana nodded, "Until you have experience, you need to use a ritual to focus and gather your power."

"Read it to me." Brian said.

"The usual stuff. Create a circle around yourself using salt or powdered quartz. The circle forms a protective barrier for your body while you are away. Sit inside the circle, then draw protection sigils around the circle's edges. Lit a candle, it should be tall enough to last through the ritual."

"Got it, then I recite the chant?" Brian asked.

"If you have an item or token related to the person, lay it near the candle. If not a personal item, at least a picture to help focus your spell. Then center yourself. Breathe deeply and envision the person asleep.

"Then what?"

"Say the incantation, close your eyes. Feel each breath drawing you away from the physical world, allow yourself to slip off solid ground and inside their dream."

"How do I return?"

"Take a deep breath and blow out the candle."

Brian nodded, "I will take this home and add it to my studies." He gently closed the book.

Morgana placed her open hand on Brian's chest. She frowned, tilting her head. She shook her head as if brushing away a thought, "I have a powerful amulet." Her voice was melodic as she removed a ring from her finger. The ring sparkled as it caught the light of the torch flames. "This is my most potent protection." Morgana placed the ring in Brian's palm.

Brian sensed a brilliant white light emanating from the ring. He turned the ring over in his hand and touched the brown gemstone in the ring's setting. "Does the power come from this stone?"

"That is not a stone, it is wood from the cross of the prophet. The ring's band is made from an iron nail used at his crucifixion."

"Seriously?" Brian looked closely. The wood is a dark, rich mahogany color with a slightly rough texture, cut in a square shape and set in a bezel setting. Simple, yet elegant. Brian closed his hand around it, it felt like his flesh never contacted the ring, vibrating with power and protected by an invisible force shield. He opened his hand and slid the ring on. His body trembled as the ring merged with him. "I can feel its power."

"Now, I need something from you."

"Anything."

"I don't ask lightly. I am getting weaker, and I must train my successor."

"You want me to be your successor?"

"No," Morgana smiled sadly, "I want your firstborn," Morgana said. "Our child will be our replacement."

"What? Wait, you want my baby? To have a baby with me?" Brian heard his heart pounding in his ears.

Morgana nodded her head, "Yes."

Brian breathed deeply, trying to slow down his heart. "Didn't we have sex already? I mean, the first time we met, the energy transfer."

"Do you think I raped you?"

"No," Brian said. "I'm sure it, I mean, I was consensual."

Morgana huffed. "We did not have sex. I siphoned a little energy from you. I needed to be sure you were the one."

"Well," Brian said with a sheepish grin. "I need to think it over."

"Unfortunately, my time is now. You're 30 years late in your time, 3,000 years in mine. I had given up hope."

Morgana untied the sash around her neck and let her gown fall to the floor. She was naked underneath. She traced her fingers over her breasts, slowly down to her pubic hair.

Brian's body flushed with desire. He wanted her. He always wanted her. His body was aflame, he wanted nothing else than to be with her. In a moment of clarity, he asked, "Did you place a spell on me?"

Morgana gently shook her head. "Bewitchment isn't consent," she answered.

"You're seducing me," Brian said, taking a step back and looking away from her beauty, toward the stone palace floor.

"I am offering a one-time-only opportunity to bond with me. If you agree, I will train our child in the arts. It's a contract, not a statement. Will you consent?"

"Morgana, you're not giving me any time to consider. I don't know how things run in Never-Never Land. Who will I be to this child? I have five years to prepare to battle Specter, and I'm you want me to add being with you and raising a child."

"You will not be with me, and the child will be mine, not ours. You can meet her, but she can never be your daughter."

"You want a sperm donor, that's not who I am."

Morgana's shoulders drooped. The soft torchlight, once flattering her porcelain features, now revealed a faint tremor in her lower lip. Even the ever-present crackle of the cold flames seemed to pause. "By this act, the fate of our two realms is in peril."

"I'm just a mortal. How can I be this important?" And then he sensed her trembling anxiety, her fear was rooted in her core. He went deeper and saw an oblivion, the stars and galaxies in the universe went black.

Morgana turned her back to him, "It's lost. I must prepare."

"Wait."

She pivoted to face him again, torchlight gleaming against tear-bright eyes

* * *

As Terry drove up to the front security gate of Sing Sing prison, Brian received a cellphone call from Detective Atwood from the 119th precinct. He had another missing child case right up Brian's alley. Brian said he would be happy to help if he could and would be back on Staten Island after lunch. They agreed to meet at Brian's house at 1:30 pm.

Terry turned into the line of cars waiting to gain entry into the prison parking lot.

Brian and Terry entered the outer gates of Sing Sing prison in Ossining, New York. A guard escorted them through building "H", passing through a few guard-protected locked doors to a waiting room at the end of a green-painted corridor. The waiting room was small, made of unadorned concrete block walls painted white. A stainless-steel table bolted to the floor was positioned in the center of the room. Four stainless steel chairs surround the table, two chairs on each side. He and Terry sat side by side at the table. The room looked cleanly scrubbed, and a tart smell of bleach and disinfectant stung his nostrils.

Fifteen minutes later, inmate Dale Oakwood, wearing an orange prison jumpsuit, was escorted into the waiting room by two guards.

He smiled at Brian and Terry. Brian could sense joy from the convict. His handcuffs were secured to a metal bar on the table, with a short length of chain that limited his movement.

"You can leave us now. What I need to say, I need to say in private," Inmate Oakwood said.

The muscular guard didn't move. He looked at Brian and Terry, "Mr. Miller, Ms. Cott, are you comfortable being left alone with him?"

Terry and Brian nodded.

The guard put his face inches away from the front of the prisoner's face, "You may have these people fooled, but I know who you are, convict."

"That's the devil talking through you, Holmes," Oakwood responded with a slight smile. "I forgive you Holms. Jesus loves you."

"Hmmph," The guard grunted.

After the guards left the room and closed the door behind them, Brian asked, "How did you get permission for me to come here?"

"I had to trade the location of dead kids I killed in exchange for this opportunity."

"Do you think I'm impressed by that? Why do you want to see me?" Brian asked.

"You're the Sovereign Sorcerer, right?"

"What's it to you?"

"You saved my life, well, indirectly. When Cantar recognized you as the Sovereign, it left my body to tell his master he had found you."

"You were possessed?" Terry gasped.

"Who's Cantar?" Brian questioned.

"A demon." Oakwood's eyes clouded with sorrow. "It's been twenty years since I was taken over, twenty kills ever since. Maybe I can do some good in my life by helping you." The inmate flipped a hidden piece of paper he had palmed toward Brian.

Brian unfolded the paper, his eyes tracing the fine lines of an ancient ruin hieroglyphic drawn on cheap prison paper. He shrugged, "What's this?"

"The master's name," the inmate replied solemnly.

Brian's mind shifted into hyperdrive, thinking of learning the Specter's name. He studied hieroglyphic letters intently, and the image shimmered like a mirage as it shifted seamlessly, transforming into pronounceable letters of the Asmodeus clan. "You called to give me this?" Brian asked.

"Yes, I only know its symbol, but the way they hid it, I figured it was important. I don't know how to put it into words, which's why I needed you to come here —to give you the symbol. I'm not a monster," Oakwood's body shook, his face twisted in pain, as he tried to control his voice from trembling as he spoke. "Me, I never hurt any child. Cantar did it. It controlled my body like a puppet and performed those disgusting, vile acts. I was trapped." He pleaded, "I was captive in my own body, forced to participate, unable to do anything, I couldn't even kill myself."

Brian swept his hand, scanning Oakwood for any sign of deceit. As far as he could determine, he was being truthful. But Brian knew there were many cloaking spells one could cast to hide intentions. Without confidence, Brian said, "I believe you."

Oakwood sagged with relief; a genuine warmth radiated from him despite the grim despair of the prison.

"But my belief will not help you or make your life easier in prison," Brian said.

"This isn't prison," Oakwood replied softly, looking around the room, "this is heaven. Prison is being bound to a demon, doing unspeakable acts with your body. Feeling it feed on the fear and pain it created was horrific."

Brian closed his eyes and nodded.

"You commuted my sentence in hell," Oakwood uttered in reverence.

"Is there anything you can tell me about Cantar's master, any weakness?" Brian asked.

"No, not that I can think of. Most of the time it was like living underwater. He only let me surface so I could experience him killing and torturing people; it increased his pleasure."

"Does the demon have any weakness or vulnerability that would help me defeat it?"

Oakwood shook his head, "No."

Brian nodded, "Is there anything I can do for you?"

Oakwood shrugged, "I study scripture and attend church daily. I do my best to follow Christ."

Brian said, "Keep walking with God, and peace will find you."

Tears of joy streamed down Dale's face, "You mean that? Thank you."

"How did you become possessed, if you don't mind me asking?" Terry spoke hesitantly.

Oakwood took a moment to reflect, his gaze focused inwardly, and he sighed deeply. I wanted the good things in life. I learned some magic rituals. You know, to increase my luck to have real estate deals break my way. It worked. So, I kept using more and more rituals. The bewitchment rituals to make women desire me were dark, I knew I was taking chances, but the women were so beautiful and the drugs and the money were too much of a high to resist. I kept practicing dark magic. I marked myself to declare my alliance. He showed Terry the satanic pentagon star burned in his forearm. "That's the Sigil of Baphomet. Soon after, Cantar had control of me."

"This could be a book. What do you think, Brian, a real story of possession?" Terry asked.

"When we met, you had a problem believing I was psychic; now, you want to write about demonic possessions?"

"I've seen some shit since then."

Oakwood thought about it, "I don't know. A book, huh? I spend my time trying to make it through the day without being beaten up. I want to serve God and contribute to society. That's what matters now."

"I think your book would do that by educating people about the dangers of the dark arts," Terry said.

Inmate Oakwood gave a bitter laugh, "Who's gonna write my book?"

"I will. I'm a writer." Terry beamed a smile at him.

Brian nodded in agreement, "A good one too. Think of it as your redemption. The souls you might save who will learn what you learned through your journey."

###

Brian and Terry returned to Staten Island and finished lunch at Brian's home around one o'clock. They discussed working on Oakwood's book, tentatively titled "Journey from Darkness."

Detective Atwood rang his doorbell at 1:30 pm. He was accompanied by policewoman Kathern Abbott from Child Services, who would take the child into custody should they successfully find her.

This case involved the kidnapping of an eight-year-old girl, Debbie Wong.

Brian's mind was thinking of the potential advantages of knowing the name of the Specter; he planned to visit Morgana as soon as this job was finished.

He pushed aside his thoughts about Oakwood and tried to listen to what the detective and Policewoman told him. He couldn't focus; he kept turning over the symbol in his mind and wondering if it was Spector's name.

The four of them squeezed into Brian's new Lincoln. Terry drove, Brian sat alongside her in the passenger seat, and the two police officers sat in the back seat. The detectives handed Brian a blouse, a rainbow unicorn necklace, and a school notebook belonging to the missing girl; he held them tight in his hands, hoping to pick up a signal from her. Brian sensed her, but instead of apprehension, he felt a calmness.

"I am sensing the girl, but it doesn't feel like she's in any danger. She's calm."

"Didn't you listen to anything we said? The girl's father kidnapped her. He doesn't have custody."

He didn't, he was preoccupied with Specter's name and Oakwood. "Atwood, something's not right with this, I can sense it."

"Let's find the girl and work out your feelings after," Atwood replied.

Forty-five minutes later, they parked their vehicle outside the JetBlue terminal, and two airport security police officers strolled beside them inside.

Detective Atwood, with a photograph in his hand, scanned every child in his vicinity while Brian scoured the Departures Screen. He spotted it—the flight to Boston was set to board in fifteen minutes at Terminal 7.

Brian turned to Atwood urgently, "Boston, terminal 7." He said, pointing toward the departure screen.

They ran to Terminal 7, and Atwood spotted Debbie Wong, sitting by a well-dressed gentleman in the waiting area. Terry and Brian watched as four police officers stormed in, their strides purposeful and menacing. The policewoman grabbed the young girl, yanking her away from her father as the policemen spun him around and handcuffed him.

Debbie Wong screamed at the top of her lungs, "Leave my daddy alone!" Her little fists flew as she fought off the policewoman, blindly thrashing in fear.

Mr. Wong shouted, "Sweetheart, stop! We tried. Go with the policewoman now, I'll work everything out with your mother."

Brian approached. He felt Mr. Wong's anxiety and panic, and the little girl's terror and sadness.

"Atwood, wait. I told you something was wrong," Brian said.

"Nothing's wrong, buddy. You're like a goddamn psychic bloodhound. I'd never believe it if I didn't see it myself."

Brian spun away from Atwood and moved closer to the young girl. The Policewoman stood in front of the girl.

"Stop right there, Mr. Miller," Abbott stated, holding up her arm.

No more Mr. Nice Guy, Brian thought, sweeping his hand in front of his stomach.

Abbott doubled over, grasping her stomach and throwing up while falling to her knees. Brian stepped around her.

"Young lady," Brian said gently. "I want to help you and your daddy. May I hold your hand for a second?"

The girl looked puzzled but slowly moved her hand to meet Brian's. Brian held her hand. Detective Atwood approached Abbott.

"Kathy, you okay?" Detective Atwood asked as policewoman Abbott continued to hold her stomach on the terminal floor. Kathern waved him off and pointed toward Brian and young Debbie Wong.

Atwood approached Brian and the young girl. "Brian, you have to step away," Detective Atwood said, "She's in our custody."

Brian turned toward Atwood. "You used me," Brian said.

"What are you talking about?" Atwood answered with indignation.

"That's her father."

"I told you that. The mom has custody. He was trying to leave the state with his daughter."

"Mom is a first-chair concert violinist who doesn't give two shits or spend time with her daughter. Debbie is her trophy child. She leaves this child with sitters, even when she's not touring. That man over there," Brian pointed toward Mr. Wong. "He cares and wants to bring her up. He wasn't kidnapping her, he was rescuing her."

"Well, aren't you a fucking wealth of information all of a sudden?"

"God damn it! I was preoccupied; I didn't get it until now. We must make this right," Brian said.

"No, we must follow the law. She's going back to her mother. The courts will decide where Debbie eventually stays. But the courts will not look too kindly on Daddy Dearest over there kidnapping his daughter."

"What can we do at this point?" Terry asked him.

"Throw money at it," Brian sighed. "Follow me," Brian said, walking toward Mr. Wong,

As Brian approached, he sensed a man lost and broken. Brian did this. "Mr. Wong, I'm Brian Miller. I made a mistake. I want to make it up to you. I'll pay for your legal fees and bail to get you released from jail. I'll continue to support you until this whole custody thing you have going on with your wife is settled."

Mr. Wong looked at Brian for a second and said, "Why? You're the one who led the police here and had me arrested. I thought you worked for my wife."

"I don't work for your wife. As I said, it was a mistake."

"Do you know who my wife is? She is the first chair of New York's Philharmonic at Lincoln Center. She can afford top lawyers. I'm an EMT at St. Vincent's Hospital. I don't have that kind of money for lawyers."

"You do now, now you have me," Brian said. "I'll pay your lawyers. To show my sincerity, my assistant Terry will transfer 30,000 dollars into your bank account for legal fees." Brian turned to Terry, "Terry, please give Mr. Wong my card."

Terry placed Brian's business card into Mr. Wong's pants pocket. Brian counted out five one-hundred-dollar bills from his wallet and stuffed the bills into Mr. Wong's other pocket.

"This money will hold you for now. Terry will find a lawyer for your arraignment. We can work out the details later."

"Why are you helping me? You don't know me?"

"You're on my path."

"Path?" Mr. Wong repeated quickly. "What path? Are you crazy?"

Brian took a big breath in and let it out slowly. "No, I'm psychic."

Mr. Wong's head jerked as if slapped; his eyes darted around the terminal like a trapped animal.

Terry stepped in front of Brian to speak to Mr. Wong. "The money is real," Terry reassured Mr. Wong in a soft, mollifying tone. "Take it. I think he's crazy, too."

Mr. Wong's agitation subsided.

Detective Atwood and the recovering Policewoman Abbott arranged to be driven back to NY with the young girl. Brian and Terry began walking out of the terminal to their car. The New Jersey cops brought Mr. Wong to the airport station for processing.

The airport terminal's automatic glass doors opened, and they walked outside. Terry said, "Are you crazy, promising Mr. Wong 30,000 dollars? You don't have that kind of money to be throwing around."

They walked to where the car was parked.

"Nonsense," Brian said. "Our movie has already booked over 20 million in three months. That's 15 million in profit. Our cut of that is about 3 million."

"No, it isn't. According to the studio, the movie hasn't turned a profit."

"That's impossible. The movie cost five million to make, and made over 20 million. Have you passed this by Larry?"

"Larry isn't an entertainment lawyer. They have some creative accounting skills in Hollywood. The 200K we received on signing is all the money we're getting from this movie."

"That has to be wrong. Larry said we signed for 20%, that's 10% each, which should be around a million and a half."

"As far as the head of the studio is concerned, our movie tanked. There are no profits."

Brian stopped walking. "He screwed us?"

"Royally," Terry answered.

As Terry drove from the terminal, Brian said, "I want you to fly out to California tomorrow and ask to meet with the studio head. Have him explain why we are not getting our cut."

"He's just going to laugh at us."

"Let him."

"I feel you, but we're just burning more money."

Two days later, Terry called Brian outside the Dalo Films building.

"I spoke to Mr. Samual Cooper, he said he would need the approval of the board of directors to change our payout for the movie. And they're not going to allow me to talk to any board members. I can catch a flight back to New York tonight."

"Who's on the board of directors for the film company?" Brian asked.

"I'm not sure."

"Stay in California. Get me pictures of the board members and their home addresses?"

"What are you planning?"

"It's too soon to say, but the pictures and addresses would help."

"Okay, I'll do that. I have been meaning to ask. What did Morgana say about the symbol Oakwood gave you?"

"It may be real, or it may be a trick. Having a wrong name is worse than having no name, she is thinking of a way to test the name without putting anyone in danger."

Around 1 pm, Brian received text messages with pictures and addresses of the board members.

"Can I come home now?" Terry pleaded on the phone.

"Yes, but if you want to stay a few days and take in the sights."

"I'm booking the next flight home," Terry said and hung up.

Brian stretched out a map of Los Angeles and placed a pin at each board member's home location. He prepared his circle, lined up his candles and waited. LA was three hours behind NY, he would need to wait twelve hours before he could expect to dream walk into someone sleeping in LA.

Samual Cooper slept in his bed. He dreamed a dream of shopping in a store. A tall man approached him, dark hair graying at the temples, bushy eyebrows, grey eyes, with a stubble beard.

"Mr. Cooper," Brian asked.

"Who are you?"

"I'm Brian Miller. I'm the guy you screwed out of money for my movie Psychic."

"Yeah, right. Your girl was in my office yesterday. Listen, kid, every virgin gets fucked in Hollywood. Consider yourself lucky, I'm the guy who popped your cherry. I only fucked you on one movie. Someone else would have fucked you on your next two movies. Relax, kid, you'll make money on your next movie."

Brian shook his head, "Hmm, I believe our deal was 20% of the profit from the money after the five million in production cost. As I see it, your company currently owes Terry and me three million dollars."

Samual Cooper laughed. "You're not hearing me, son. That's not happening."

The world swirled around them. Samual Cooper found himself standing on a four-foot square concrete platform two thousand feet above his home in Santa Monica.

The frigid air whipped, causing him to sway and almost lose his balance. Brian Miller hovered ten feet in front of Samual. Dark clouds filled the sky. A full moon peeked through the clouds and illuminated the slowly shrinking platform.

Samual's eyes widened as he looked at the diminishing platform, "Hey, this is a dream, right?"

"Right," Brian answered him.

Samual punched his thigh. "Wake up!" He hit himself harder. "Wake up.."

"Try this," Brian suggested as a sledgehammer materialized in Samual's hand.

Samual lifted the sledgehammer above his head and brought it down with great force on the side of his knee. His knee popped inward, and he collapsed on impact. Samual howled in pain.

Brian laughed.

The world swirled around them again, and when it stopped, they floated above an active Icelandic volcano. Lava flowed down the mountain.

"My knee is broken. I need medical attention." Samual cried.

"Don't be ridiculous. This is a dream."

"No, it can't be. This is too real. The heat is unbearable, and the sulfur is suffocating me. Fly us up higher."

"That's not the plan. Nope, in fact it's going to get a lot hotter for you when I drop you into that lava. I figure I'll let you cook for a minute or so, then I'll pull you out. Once you're turned into a crispy critter, maybe you'll have a change of heart."

"No, wait, don't do that shit," Samual pleaded. "What the fuck do you want?"

"My twenty percent."

"It's not up to me. The board must approve that expenditure. It must pass a majority vote. I'm only one vote on the board."

"You'll contact the other board members in the morning and start the vote."

"Anything you say."

"Listen to me, Sam, this is important."

Samual nodded.

"Keep your word to me this time. If I must revisit you, I will put you in a dungeon and have five trolls torture you for five years. By the time you wake up in the morning, you'll be babbling so incoherently that your family will have you committed to a mental institution. You got me?"

"I got it."

The world swirled around them, and they returned to the mall store. Brian bowed and disappeared. Samual Cooper woke and jumped out of bed. His leg had a severe cramp, and his heart raced. As he rubbed and straightened out his leg, he wondered if what had just happened was real. He wasn't taking any chances with that fucking psychic psycho bastard. He would call the board tomorrow and ask for a vote to provide the 20%

compensation to Miller and Cott. I'll say it's for creating a good relationship with them for their next goddamn movie. I can sell that. He tried to calm down and stop his heart from racing, but he couldn't. His wife slept in their bed unaware. Sleep for him was out of the question, and he settled on his living room sofa, waiting for the morning to call the other board members.

In Staten Island, Brian blew out the candle and checked his watch. It took him less than five minutes to convince Samual Cooper to honor their deal. He expected it would take longer. He looked at the next board member on his list and checked his map.

An hour later, only two board members were left on his list. Ty Wilson was next.

Brian lit the next candle, stared at the photograph, meditated, and fell into Ty Wilson's mind.

"Who fucking dares?" A voice boomed and echoed through the canyons of a primeval hellscape.

Brian's heart seized. The last time he sensed this magnitude of evil was his encounter with Specter. A black demon materialized before him. He stood twelve feet, massive horns protruding from its forehead, claw feet with glowing, sinister red eyes. The ground trembled as the demon stepped forward.

The demon crouched down to look closer at Brian, hissing with a forked tongue, it said, "Sorcerer."

Brian tried to release himself from Ty Wilson's mind, but couldn't control his body in his den to blow out the candle; he was trapped. Brian stepped backward, putting some distance between himself and the beast. His pulse pounded in his ear.

The demon began circling its arms, gathering balls of green luminescent energy around its arms. The energy crackled with power.

Brian had no weapon to fight the beast. Had Morgana foreseen this? Had she given him the ring for this moment? Clenching his right fist, he pressed his lips against the ring and kissed it and murmured, "By the wood of the cross and the blood of the sacrament."

The demon screeched and shot a violent burst of green fire at Brian.

He didn't think-he acted. He lunged forward, driving his fist into the oncoming blaze. His ring reflected the blast back toward the monster. The demon took the hit in its chest, and its force knocked it on its back.

The demon flailed on the ground, writhing in pain, floundering. The distorted world flickered, like static on a broken television. It's mind lost its grip on the dreamscape, Brian felt his body again, and blew out the candle. The dreamscape fell out of view, replaced with the interior of his den and the smoldering candle, its final wisps of smoke curling into the air.

Brian stood. His protection ring was burning hot and throbbing. "That was close," Brian muttered under his breath. He exhaled sharply, steadying himself. "No more dream walking tonight."

Morgana's Shop – A Meeting of Minds

The drive to the south side of Staten Island was a blur. The streets were deserted at this hour, the dim streetlights barely illuminating the blind alley where he sensed Morgana's shop hid in the shadows.

He found the entrance between two forgotten storefronts. The air inside carried the scent of dried herbs and aged parchment.

Morgana was already waiting for him, seated at her round table adorned with symbols etched into the wood. Without a word, Brian sat across from her.

"It was wise to escape while you had the chance," Morgana said, her voice smooth yet laced with quiet amusement.

Brian met her gaze, irritation simmering beneath his exhaustion. "Did you see this happening tonight?"

Morgana tilted her head slightly. "It was a strong probability."

His fists clenched. "Then why the hell didn't you warn me?"

The flickering candlelight cast sharp shadows across her face. "Because then you wouldn't learn what you must learn."

Brian scowled. "I came pretty damn close to losing my life."

Morgana raised an eyebrow, unfazed. "So, it's a lesson you won't forget."

"You could have just told me the damn lesson!" he snapped.

"And you would have ignored it," she countered. "It would not carry the same weight as being trapped in a dream by one of the Specter's minions."

Brian exhaled sharply, dragging a hand down his face. "So you nearly let me die just to prove a point?"

Morgana leaned forward, her gaze dark and unwavering. "You're playing a larger game, Brian. You think these events are personal, that they only pertain to you. They don't."

She placed a hand over her stomach, fingers tracing protective circles. "You are the protector of your realm. If it falls, billions of souls are lost. But we are fortunate. Very fortunate."

Brian's blood ran cold. He knew what was coming before she even said it.

"We have a scion."

His breath caught in his throat. "My child."

Morgana inclined her head in a slow nod. "She is the Eighth Sovereign, destined to protect this realm."

A mix of emotions twisted inside him—pride, confusion, resentment. "Then I'm not needed anymore?"

Morgana let out a low chuckle. "Oh, you are very much needed. For the next century, at least. While the Eighth Sovereign trains under me, you must keep your realm intact."

She tapped a long, painted fingernail against the table. "But I cannot protect you from your own foolish decisions. The Dreamscape was not your first reckless act. You nearly drained your entire life force curing Cheryl's addiction. You make yourself weak. And weakness, vulnerability invites attacks."

Brian inhaled deeply, as her words sank in.

"You are the Sovereign Sorcerer," Morgana said, her voice like steel wrapped in silk. "Start acting like it. Keep fit. Stay powerful. Stay protected."

Brian nodded, begrudgingly. "You're right."

Morgana smirked. "Of course I'm right."

Brian rubbed his temple, still processing everything. "What could I have done differently before entering the dreamscape?"

Morgana's lips curled into a knowing smile. "Weapons. You have much to learn. There are spells to summon the flaming sword of Archangel Michael, Apollo's bow, Thunderbolts, Thor's hammer... many more."

Brian's brows furrowed. "You mean all the weapons from mythology?"

"Mythology," she repeated with a scoff. "What you call myths, I call history. The weapons exist, Brian. Calling them is easy. Wielding them, however, is an entirely different matter."

Brian exhaled, shaking his head. "Proficiency with weapons take years. I don't have that much time."

Morgana's smile widened. "Agreed. Which is why you should spend most of your time here."

Brian narrowed his eyes. "What are you suggesting?"

She tapped the table. "Time flows differently here in my realm. Five years in the lower realm is five hundred years here. If you visit here often, you can train properly. I need you to succeed, Brian."

A flicker of insight flared in his mind. "So you can stop hiding from the Specter? Stop moving your portal so it can't find you?"

Morgana's smile didn't falter. "Among other things."

Brian sat back, mulling over the offer.

"Have you spoken to Terry about your future?" Morgana asked.

Brian hesitated. "No."

"Then it's time. She is on your path. Terry should join you here in my realm."

Brian grimaced. "I don't think that's a good idea. She might... flip out."

Morgana chuckled. "Remember Pinocchio? The animated film you loved as a child?"

Brian nodded, unsure where she was going with this.

"Jiminy Cricket."

He frowned. "Yeah, what about him?"

Morgana's expression turned serious. "Terry is your Jiminy Cricket, Brian. You left her vulnerable. The demon knows her now. She inquired at the production company. She's no longer just an observer."

Brian's stomach clenched.

Morgana turned her head to the right, looking out. "They found her, Brian; evil forces are gathering around her house. You need to get there and protect her."

Brian stood. "I'll leave now, I can get there in half an hour."

"She doesn't have half an hour. When you walk out my door, you will be in front of Terry's house."

"Really?"

"I can do small things, hurry"

Brain walked out the shop's door and found himself in front of Terry's side entrance door. He placed his hand over the doorknob and willed the tumblers to turn and unlock.

Not wanting to wake Terry, he cast a protection spell over the house, then lay down on her couch. If anything came in for her, they would have to get passed him first.

At 6:30 in the morning, Brian's cell phone rang from an unknown number.

He answered. "Hello?"

A guttural growl slithered through the line. Then a sneering voice. "Sorcerer. Why the fuck did you run? We were just getting started."

Brian's lips curled into a smirk. "Hi, Ty. I had more important things to do."

Ty Wilson snarled. "I smelled your fear. You ran."

Brian let out a dry laugh. "I had bigger fish to fry. You weren't much of a challenge. I knocked you on your ass in two seconds. Next time, I'll shove Poseidon's Trident so far up your ass, it'll double as a lightning rod then I'll stomp on your face to improve your looks."

He growled, "Mock me at your peril, human." A click.

He hoped he sounded more confident than he felt. Brian tossed the phone onto the coffee table and stood up from Terry's couch. He slept on worse.

A few minutes later, the soft creak of stairs announced Terry's descent. She padded down, her hair tousled from sleep, wearing an oversized hoodie that barely covered her gym shorts. The moment she spotted Brian, her brows knitted together in confusion.

Her expression darkened. "What are you doing here? And how the hell did you get in?"

Brian rubbed the back of his neck. "They know who you are Terry. I needed to protect you."

Terry folded her arms, eyes narrowing. "Go on."

He hesitated, then explained that because she made the inquiry at Dalo studios, the evil force identified her, and began the conversation about having a child with Morgana.

"It's complicated."

"Oh, I bet it is." She leaned forward, her voice edged with something sharp. "You having a child with some—what did you call her?—outer-worldly being?"

"My child will be her successor in the library."

Terry cocked her head. "She's a librarian?"

Brian let out a dry chuckle. "No, Terry. She's a seer. The library is more than books. It's a vault of knowledge, magic, and fate."

Terry pressed her lips into a thin line. "And you're just... okay with this?"

"I didn't have much of a choice, the fate of realms hung in the balance. Morgana needed to conceive at that moment. She wished she had more time, but I was thirty years late in showing up."

Terry's fingers curled into fists. "So, what now? You're a father, married or not. You'll be raising this child together."

Brian shook his head. "No. All I can do is visit. Time moves differently in her realm. She'll give birth in about a week from our perspective. In a month, the child will be a toddler."

Terry's expression twisted, something unreadable flashing across her face—anger, frustration, maybe something deeper. "Why didn't you stay? Why didn't you marry her?" Her voice dripped with sarcasm and barely restrained emotion.

Brian met her gaze steadily. "Because I'm destined to marry someone else."

Terry let out a sharp laugh, shaking her head. "Great. And what's that skank's name?"

Brian inhaled slowly. "Terry. Her name is Terry."

Terry's breath hitched. The sharpness in her expression melted into something unguarded, uncertain. "Me?"

Brian nodded. "Morgana said it's a thick branch on the tree of probabilities."

Terry snorted, rubbing her temples. "Is there any fruit on that tree? Jesus, now I'm starting to talk like you. I mean—kids. Do we have kids?"

Brian shrugged. "I didn't ask." He sensed the shift in her tone - excitement, anticipation.

Terry exhaled, shaking her head. "We have to talk."

Brian moved closer. "We can talk all day if you want. But not here. My house is better protected. We should go there."

Terry hesitated.

"Pack what you need," Brian urged. "I want you to move in with me. It's the only way I can keep you safe."

Her lips parted slightly, and for the first time since this conversation began, there was no sarcasm, no resistance. Just a quiet understanding.

Terry nodded.

The next day Terry paced into Brian's den, her phone clutched in her hand. Her breath came fast, excitement buzzing in her voice. "I just got a call from Dalo Studios."

Brian looked up from his chair, where he had been absently turning Morgana's ring on his finger. "Yeah?"

"They're allocating three million dollars in royalties to be deposited into our bank accounts."

He sighed, shaking his head. "Nice."

Terry's expression sobered. She studied him for a long moment, the weight of the last few days pressing down on both of them. "You don't sound happy. One point five million dollars just dropped into your lap, and you look like someone kicked your dog."

Brian exhaled, rubbing his temple. "I'm afraid, Terry." He met her gaze. "For us. We're traveling a dangerous road."

Terry crossed the room and sat beside him, close enough for their shoulders to brush. Her voice softened. "You're not traveling alone anymore."

She placed her hand over his, steady and sure. "I'm with you. We'll face it together. Okay?"

Brian looked down at their hands—her warmth, her presence, her certainty.

He had even more to fight for - he had Terry. Slowly, he nodded. "Okay."

If you like this book, please leave a review.

https://www.amazon.com/review/create-review?&asin=B0CJPLK1GL

Book 2 - Chapter 1 Teacher

Brian waited at the kitchen table. A normal breakfast at home, something he hadn't enjoyed in a year. In Morgana's realm, he had lived a full year, though only a week had passed in the real world.

Terry had finished writing her next book, *Reunion*. Her publisher would be in for quite the surprise. As for Brian, he had spent the last year under Morgana's watchful eye, training in the arts.

He frowned. Terry was lingering at the front door too long.

A chill crawled up his spine as he rose from the table. The moment he stepped into the living room, he sensed it.

Brian sprinted toward the door.

One step outside the door, Terry stood frozen, unprotected. A demon had ensnared her in its thrall, siphoning away her life force.

Brian inhaled sharply, his power surged in his back, his fingers focused to a point. Ectoplasm gathered around his arm, the air crackled with spectral energy. The plasma solidified into a jagged spear, it launched, the air shrieking as ripped toward the demon.

The spear entered the demon's chest. It's trailing line curling around its torso and snaking up its throat.

The demon jerked back, snarling. Brian tightened his grip, locking the ectoplasmic binding fast.

"Release her!" Brian twisted his fist, cinching the ectoplasmic noose tighter.

The demon screeched. The tendrils burrowed into its decaying flesh, clawing at its essence. Its struggles slowed. **"Mercy, Sovereign." The words rasped from its throat. "I did not know she was yours."**

Terry gasped awake. Her eyes widened at the sight of the frail old woman, writhing in Brian's grasp.

"Brian, what are you doing?" she cried, stepping forward. "This woman needs our help!"

"Show yourself," he commanded. The response was immediate. A stench hit Terry before her eyes registered the change, the gut-wrenching reek of rot and decay. Her stomach lurched. The old woman twisted and reassembled, **her disguise dissolving into rotting limbs and sunken, lifeless eyes.**

Terry staggered, choking on bile. She leapt through the open doorway, retreating into the safety of the house.

The demon groaned, its hollow gaze locked onto Brian. "I released her, Sovereign. Returned what I took. Mercy – release me. You will never see me again."

Brian's grip didn't loosen. "No mercy."

The demon writhed. "A trade, Sovereign."

Brian's eyes narrowed. "You have nothing I want."

The demon hesitated. "Spare me, and I'll release a young girl's soul I own."

A vision flashed through Brian's mind—a young African girl convulsing on the dirt floor of a thatched hut, white foam spilling from her lips.

"She's mine," the demon hissed. "Release me and I will let her go. Refuse, and her soul is mine forever."

Brian exhaled slowly. "Release her, and I'll release you."

Miles away, in a remote North African village, the girl's convulsions ceased. Her chest rose—her first steady breath in three months. The voices were gone. Her mind was her own again.

Brian unclenched his fist. The binding dissolved, a glowing sigil burning on the demon's chest. Then it vanished.

"What was that?" Terry asked.

"A lesser demon."

"I can still smell it. That's the most disgusting thing I've ever smelled in my life."

"Why did it come here, to attack us?"

"They're testing me. Probing my strength."

"Did you pass?"

"You need more protection bindings. I'll craft binding from your garments, written sigils infused with the waters from Athena."

"My amulet doesn't work anymore?"

"Not if you're not wearing it, no."

Terry's hand found her neck bare; she had taken the amulet off to shower and forgotten to put it back on.

They walked back into the kitchen together, the air still heavy with the demon's stench and the static discharge of ectoplasma.

"This feels like only the beginning," Terry said.

Brian nodded. "I must visit Morgana for her advice. I thought I had more time, but we can lay low here. No active cases to work."

"We have this." Terry handed Brian an open envelope from the counter.

Brian unfolded the paper, it was an invoice from his lawyer representing Mr. Wong in his custody battle.

"Fifty grand -- for two weeks' work."

"I'm sure more bills are to come."

Brian studied the invoice closely. "Her attorney, Mr. Dershowitz is burning up my money in legal fees for unnecessary work." He set the paper down, his mind already churning. "I think it's time we had a little chat with Ms. Wong and her attorney. On our terms."

Terry raised an eyebrow. "What are you thinking?"

"Dream walking."

At 1:00 a.m., the alarm dragged Brian and Terry out of bed. Terry brewed a pot of coffee while Brian prepared his den for dream walking, laying out photographs and addresses for both Ms. Wong and Mr. Dershowitz.

Finishing their coffee, Terry asked, "Are you sure you can reach out to me if something goes wrong?"

"I'm as sure as I can be. If you hear me call your name, douse the candle after repeating the protection chant."

Brian checked his ward: the ring, sigils on each wrist, and another on the back of his shirt. He was as ready as he could be. Terry was his anchor to the waking world; ready to pull him back if the dreamscape went wrong.

Brian circled Ms. Wong, scanning her for any trace of malevolence. Finding none, he slipped into her dream. He entered a vast concert hall where Ms. Wong stood center stage, bow sliding across her violin. Elaborate chandeliers swayed above her to a wind that didn't exist, hanging from a ceiling that wasn't there.

"Cathy, can we talk?"

Ms. Wong looked up at Brian, "I recognize you. You're helping my husband. This is a dream, isn't it?"

"Yes, it is." Brian realized interaction snapped the dreamer into lucidity.

"What do you want?" Ms. Wong asked, putting down her violin and standing.

"I wanted to discuss the possibility of you dropping the case against your husband and granting him custody of Debbie."

"You're crazy. Mind your own fucking business. This has nothing to do with you. You are a meddler. I know what's best for my family."

The thought of dangling her over a volcano surged through him, but he forced a breath to center himself. "Your path is your choice. I am only here to show its cost to those around you."

"Are you deaf or just stupid—or both?"

Brian ignored her. "This is how your daughter feels about being separated from her father." He channeled Debbie's raw emotions from Newark Airport directly into Cathy.

Cathy doubled over in grief. "Oh no… Stop. I don't want to feel this."

Brian withdrew Debbie's feelings from Ms. Wong. "And this is how your husband felt when his daughter was taken from him." He drove Mr. Wong's anguish and hopelessness into her.

Cathy fell to her knees and started crying. "Please stop. I've done nothing to you—why are you doing this?"

"I am trying to help you."

"How is causing me this pain helping? I want what's best for Debbie. With me Debbie will be surrounded by art and music where she can flourish. What can my husband provide? A cramped shitty apartment in Queens, community college and a dead end EMT job, he'll never be more than that."

"He offers his love and his time. It's not the quality of time that matters, it's the time itself. And he gives all of it. Here is your future if you don't change. This is how Debbie will feel toward you twenty years from now."

Debbie's thoughts flooded into her, and Cathy sobbed. "She hates me… She despises Charlie for not saving her… *It's not my fault. My career demands travel and availability. I couldn't spend the time with her. Oh my God. This cannot be true.*"

"It doesn't have to be. Here's an alternative future."

In Cathy's mind, Debbie beamed on her wedding day, joy radiating as friends and family encircled her. The warmth of her daughter's love poured into her.

"Yes… this is the future I want."

"Then end the custody battle. He will grant generous visitation, as she grows older, she can even accompany you on summer tours."

"I will do this… I'll talk to my lawyer tomorrow…"

Brian dissolved from her dream and returned to Staten Island, where he blew out the candle to end the dream walk.

"How did it go?" Terry asked.

"Not bad. I think I was able to change her perspective regarding the custody."

"And you managed it without the volcano?" Terry teased.

Brian smirked. "Yes, without the volcano. Now hand me the lawyer's picture."

"If Cathy's on board, do you really need to convince her lawyer too?"

"Lawyers thrive on conflict. I don't want him persuading her to change her mind."

With a sigh, Terry handed Brian the photograph. Brian studied the photo while Terry replaced the candle. At his nod, she lit it and sat beside him, listening as he began the dream walker's mantra.

Larry Dershowitz was buying a hot dog at Coney Island. The aroma of grilled onions and sizzling sausages filled the air. The salty sea breeze rustled Brian's hair as he entered the dreamscape. Brian's form blurred, then reshaped into that of Larry's deceased mother, Anna.

"Larele," Brian called, projecting his voice with the tender lilt of Larry's memory of his mother's affection.

Larry froze, the hot dog slipped from his hand as he spun around. "Momma?"

"Bubbeleh," Brian said, his expression warm, his arms outstretched.

With tears welling in his eyes, Larry dashed across the timeworn wooden boardwalk to embrace his mother. "I've missed you so much, Momma."

Brian held him close, then slowly pulled back from Larry's embrace, cupping Larry's face with his hands, he spoke softly. "I only have a little time to talk, boychik."

"Talk? Talk about what, Momma?"

"This man, Charlie Wong—you are speaking ill of him, twisting the truth to paint him as a bad father."

"I'm a lawyer." He said defensively. "I am representing my client, who is his spouse. That's how I win cases."

"This time, bubbeleh, you will not twist the truth." Anna said, her voice resonant and wise. Lifting her gaze, she pointed to the sky. "This man is connected."

"He's connected… to God?" Larry whispered, his eyes widening in awe.

"We all are, darling."

"I will do anything you want, Momma. Tell me what you want. You want me to throw the case out? It's out. Lose it? It's lost. What do you want?" Larry asked eagerly.

"Talk to your client. Reason with her. Show her that ending the fight and letting Debbie stay with her father is best for them all."

"Okay… I don't know if she'll do that. She might just fire me."

"Then she will live with the consequences of that decision, not you."

"Not me," Larry echoed, relief in his voice.

"Until we meet again, boychik," Anna said.

"Don't go. Talk to me some more."

"My time is up." Anna blew her son a kiss.

Brian blew out the candle in his den, dissolving from Larry's dream.

"How did this one go?" Terry asked.

"Better than expected. Gentle persuasion can work as well as force."

"Good," Terry agreed.

On Tuesday morning Brian and Terry arrived at the Queens County Courthouse on Queens Boulevard. The building's limestone facade was worn, its broad steps ascending to heavy bronze doors. Inside, the air was thick with the scent of polished wood and old paper, an almost sacred stillness punctuated by the murmur of lawyers and clients strategizing in the hallways.

The courtroom itself was a grand but aging chamber, lined with dark oak panels, high ceilings, and rows of worn wooden benches stretching toward the front, where the judge's elevated seat stood. Flanking the bench were the American and New York State flags.

To one side, at the plaintiff's table, Cathy Wong sat with her fingers wrapped around a pen she had no intention of using. Across from her at the defense table, Charlie Wong fidgeted with his tie, his fingers trembling slightly as they adjusted the knot.

And then, with the creak of an opening side door, the judge entered.

"All rise," the bailiff said.

Brian turned to Terry, lowering his voice. "We'll see how good my persuasion held..." But Terry's eyes were closed, her head dipped. She was fast asleep.

Gently, he shook Terry's shoulder. "Terry," he whispered. She remained unresponsive.

        Alarm surged through him. He checked her neck, she had a pulse. She was wearing her protection amulet, thank God and three protection sigils sewn into her undergarments. What could be attacking her? He pressed his protection ring to her hand and whispered an invocation. Nothing. Panic tightened his chest—he would have to dream walk without the ritual. His heart pounded. Don't jump in blind "Just hold on," he whispered in Terry's ear. He renewed the protection, creating an aura around himself and Terry, binding her to him. He touched Terry's face, slipping through the veil into her dream.

The hellscape unfolded with the abruptness of a nightmare. Ty Wilson's world was familiar—jagged obsidian cliffs pierced the sky, spiking up from rivers of molten rock. Sulfuric fumes choke the air. Terry hung naked, above a pit of fire, arms and legs spread wide, bound by invisible chains. Flames licked her feet, yet she didn't scream; her skin remained untouched.

Brian crashed on a nearby ledge, knees buckling as a wave of heat seared him. He rushed forward, ignoring the burning sensation in the soles of his feet.

"Terry, are you okay?" he shouted over the roar of flames.

She turned her head, her neck straining against invisible bonds. "I… I can't move. But I'm not hurt. Not yet."

A deep, snarling chuckle rolled across the infernal landscape. From the swirling smoke, Ty Wilson's towering demon with horns like twisted iron and a gaze of smoldering embers emerged.

About the Author

John Iovine is a prolific author, inventor, and entrepreneur whose work bridges the worlds of science, technology, and imagination. Over the course of his career, he has written more than a dozen books covering topics as diverse as microcontrollers, holography, Kirlian photography, artificial intelligence, and parapsychology. His ability to transform complex subjects into clear, engaging material has earned him recognition among hobbyists, students, and professionals alike.

Beyond books, John has contributed hundreds of articles to leading publications—including *Scientific American*, *Make Magazine*, *Nuts and Volts*, *Servo Magazine*, *Circuit Cellar*, and *Popular Electronics*. His writing is driven by a passion for making science accessible, inspiring curiosity, and empowering readers to explore technology hands-on.

As an innovator, John holds several U.S. patents in holography and related fields, reflecting his inventive spirit and dedication to pushing boundaries. He is also the founder of Images Scientific Instruments Inc., where he develops and manufactures scientific instruments such as Geiger counters, random number generators, and spark detectors—devices that serve both academic research and cutting-edge explorations into consciousness and the unknown.

In addition to his technical writing, John has turned his creative energy toward fiction, penning paranormal and science fiction stories that weave scientific concepts with imaginative storytelling. This dual path—fact and fiction—highlights his lifelong mission: to explore, question, and share knowledge in all its forms.

He lives in New York City with his wife, their two children, a spirited dog named Nigel, and a mischievous cat named Squeaks.